P9-EDF-154

Bodies at Sea

ILLINOIS SHORT FICTION

A list of books in the series appears at the end of this volume.

Erin McGraw

Bodies at Sea

UNIVERSITY OF ILLINOIS PRESS

Urbana and Chicago

For Todd and for Chakka

Publication of this work was supported in part by grants from the Illinois Arts Council, a state agency.

I would like to thank DePauw University and Kalamazoo College for the support they provided for the writing of some of these stories.

This book is printed on acid-free paper.

"Accepted Wisdom," first published in *The North American Review*, vol. 272, no. 4, 1987
"Testimonial" first appeared in *California Quarterly*, no. 32/33, 1988
"Life Drawing," first published in *The Georgia Review*, vol. 40, no. 2, 1986
"Talk Show," first published in *Crazyhorse*, Spring 1987
"Bodies at Sea," first published in *The Georgia Review*, vol. 41, no. 1, 1987
"A Thief," first published in *The Kenyon Review*, Spring 1989
"Tule Fogs," first published in *The Laurel Review*, Winter 1989
"The Punch-Up Man," first published in *Beloit Fiction Journal*, October 1988
"Until It Comes Closer," first published in *The Georgia Review*, vol. 42, no. 3, 1988

Library of Congress Cataloging-in-Publication Data

McGraw, Erin, 1957–
    Bodies at sea / Erin McGraw.
        p.   cm.—(Illinois short fiction)
    ISBN 0–252–01631–9 (alk. paper)
    I. Title.   II. Series.
PS3563.C3674B6   1989
813'.54—dc19   88–34288
                                          CIP

But there are perils in living always in vision—
Always inventing entire whatever paves
Or animates the innocent sand or snow
Of a mere locale.

—Robert Pinsky
An Explanation of America

Contents

Accepted Wisdom

McPherson liked to claim that the day Anne clipped him over the ear with the teapot and left for the train station was the happiest day of his life. Their marriage had been noisy, violent—he never knew when he would come home to a squalid house, shattered dinnerware strewn from kitchen to bedroom. "The woman was born to make man fear the afterlife," McPherson said to anyone who would listen the day after Anne caught the train and left Pennsylvania for good.

For a week after she left, McPherson and his daughter, Nora, crept through the house, startling each other around corners, jumping at slight sounds. In the still nights McPherson lay rigid, waiting every minute for Anne to reappear and let fly with whatever fragile object was handy. In the mornings and evenings he made one cheese sandwich after another for himself and his daughter. Then, one afternoon, Nora abruptly asked her father what he would like for supper.

"Truffles and pheasant under glass," he said.

"How about stew?" she said. "I'm tired of eating sandwiches."

Nora was thirteen. How could McPherson have been expected to know she could make a stew?

"Give me some money," she said. "I'll need to go to Hays' to get meat. We're out of bread, too. What do you want to bring for lunch tomorrow?" McPherson, slightly dazed, gave her everything in his wallet.

It seemed to take no time. "Top of her class," he bragged to the miners, to Hannah, "and nothing she can't do. Roasts! How many girls could make their dads a roast? She's got Hays so he calls her when the good meat comes in." He was seeing his daughter for the first time, and he could scarcely believe his good fortune. He was careful with her, as gentle as a suitor, thinking she was his reward for the terrible years with Anne.

"Your mother," he told Nora once, "was—unstable." Nora watched him as she always did, her large eyes taking him in, and he stopped, knowing he'd sounded foolish. What should he have told her? The last night, in their bed, Anne had whispered, "You made me crawl over glass for you. I'll make you crawl for me." What could you tell a girl about a mother like that? And Nora Anne's own daughter, though it hardly seemed believable.

Anne was gone nearly a year before she sent for Nora. By then McPherson's life with his daughter was quiet and orderly, and he found that he looked forward to returning to her from Hannah's every night. As the summer came on they watched the blue shadow from the tower at the switching yard advance across the garden. "I can give my daughter now what she has always needed," Anne had written. "I can teach her the things she needs to know."

"Ha," said McPherson. The girl didn't need to know what Anne could teach her. It was a week before he managed to tell Nora about the letter, and only then because he was afraid Anne would write again, or worse, telephone. "It would be just like her, the she-devil," McPherson told Hannah. "Just when I've got my life cleaned of her messes."

On Thursday night, while he and Nora were sitting on the screen porch and waiting for the sweet twilight air, McPherson said, "Your mother has written a letter."

"Is she well?"

Hannah would have said, "Is she still throwing things?" McPherson peered at Nora's serene profile; it was lovely and pure, and revealed nothing.

"She says she's well." What she'd in fact said was that she had finally achieved some tiny measure of happiness after the years of drudgery with McPherson, but he saw no point in sharing this.

"Is she coming back?"

"I don't think so." Not that he'd have her, as he'd told Hannah. Even a man like McPherson, notoriously soft on women, had to draw the line somewhere. There was relief in this life without jars exploding against kitchen and bedroom walls. He studied Nora for some minute sign, a direction to proceed. Her face was steady as a face on a coin. *She couldn't be missing her,* he thought. *If she cared at all, she'd be all over me for everything the she-devil said. It was only polite to ask.* "She said she misses you," he said.

Nora kept looking into the cooling evening air. "But not enough to come home."

"No. She didn't talk about coming home."

Nora remained quiet for a long time. McPherson watched the shadow gain three pickets. She had always been her father's girl, everyone could see it. Any daughter of Anne's would have taken off like a banshee. Nora was steady, like her dad. She planned ahead for things, asking him Sunday what he'd like to eat Thursday. She mended the china bowls and knickknacks that Anne had left demolished in her wake. "I wish she'd come home," Nora said.

"She wants you to join her," McPherson said before he could stop himself. In the deepening air Nora's face was luminous, and he rushed on. "She's living in California. She works in a bank. Her house has an avocado tree in back." And a lawyer inside, Anne had added for McPherson's benefit, whose manliness was such that she craved him several times a day. They bedded, she said, on ripe avocados.

"She rides a bicycle to work." He and Hannah had laughed themselves weak at the notion of Anne pedaling ferociously to her office—"Gangway!" they had roared. But watching Nora's transfixed face, McPherson could find no humor. Her eyes were large and still, and he had no idea what she might be remembering, imagining. California, after all, and Nora sitting with him so still and lovely. His own daughter and he couldn't tell if she was thinking of leaving him.

"Why?" Nora asked.

"Why?" It was a good question. For all the talk of avocados, Anne had never explained why, and why now, she wanted Nora. "Well, why would a mother want her daughter to be with her? She misses you." He should perhaps have also said *She loves you,* but there was only so much that he felt fairness obliged of him.

"She left you," Nora said.

"Yes," McPherson said, alarmed enough now to be cagey with his words.

"She doesn't want you to come."

"No." Would, she said, escort him off her property with the tip of a knife—but no need to tell Nora, no need.

"What would I do in California?" Nora asked, still gazing into the blue yard.

McPherson was having trouble catching his breath. He felt a wrenching deep in his body, as if the thread—unexpectedly slender—that moored him were being battered by heavy seas. "Go to school," he said. "The beach is there. Help your mother around the house." What else could he say? Should he tell her she would meet movie stars?

After a long pause throughout which McPherson had to heave air into his lungs, she asked, "What would you do without me?"

It was the time to explain how special their relationship was. She couldn't want him to come home at night to a cold house, a silent one. She couldn't leave him alone, lighting lamps from room to room. His lips began to move, testing words softly while Nora waited. Unbidden, he thought of the rare mornings he rose before she did. In sleep she looked tender, her hair spilling across the sheets. She slept tidily, sometimes murmuring into her pillow. There was always the scent of warm skin and soap. "I don't know," he said. "I can't bear to think of it."

When Hannah asked him, as she often did, what he would do if she never let him in again, he said things like, "I'd shimmy down the chimney and come into your bedroom like Santa Claus."

"Watch I don't light a fire under you."

"I know all about your fires," he said.

Hannah lived exactly halfway between McPherson's front door and the gate outside the loading yard. Often in the summer he would leave his own house early, to eat strawberries with Hannah for breakfast. She was happy on those warm mornings, and had every window in her small house flung wide. As a result she had to keep shushing McPherson when he teased her and held her and attempted to balance strawberries on top of her breasts. "They can hear you in the next county," she said.

"It's good for them. They should remember what it was like before they all started acting like bankers. Everybody," he brayed out the window, "should be eating strawberries."

He brought her things—clusters of wisteria whose scent flooded the house, pictures and coupons from magazines. Before Anne had left he used to bring lettuce and broccoli from the garden, but after Nora took over he felt odd. Only once did he bring her a cabbage that Nora didn't seem to know what to do with. "You shouldn't have brought me this," Hannah said.

"It was extra. No sacrifice."

"Still, Nora's garden. For God's sake."

Occasionally, when McPherson and Nora were out walking, they passed Hannah on the street. McPherson held his breath and looked at the tops of trees on these occasions. "Hello, Miss Crawley," Nora would say.

"Nora. Mac."

McPherson would dip his head just in time to see Hannah's cool smile slide over him, and would smile in return, a shambling, weak thing.

"How are you getting on?" Hannah would say to Nora.

"Well, thanks. People are kind—Hays is always saving me special cuts."

"You must be his most special customer," Hannah said.

Nora looked down and smiled. "The garden's coming along now," she said. "I don't know what to do with all our cabbage— Dad says he'll go green if he eats any more." McPherson, back to looking at high branches, winced at the delicate seriousness of his daughter's voice.

"Always too much cabbage. My own father used to complain. I have a recipe for cabbage soup you might try."

"You're sure that's wise?" McPherson blurted. "Giving the girl your own recipes, I mean." Nora and Hannah wheeled to look at him, and he danced back a few steps in the dusty street. "My mother'd die before she gave out a recipe, you know."

"I don't mind sharing a cabbage recipe," Hannah said, and Nora laughed.

At such times McPherson had horrifying visions. The girl, so serious and cordial, had no idea. Hannah, that forthright woman. He imagined them over the teapot in the kitchen, talking. The two looking up at him, maybe lobbing a handy saucer.

Nora often watched Hannah as she went on her way. "I like Miss Crawley," she said once with unusual vehemence. "She's better than anyone else."

"How are your studies coming?" McPherson asked. "There's nothing more important than education."

It was only once he'd felt the urge to ask Nora if she knew anything, if people had talked at the laundry or Hays', a day when Hannah had come down the street bright as flowers, and it was all McPherson could do not to slip his arm into the nook of her waist. "There aren't many like her," he'd sighed after they parted.

"She's pretty," Nora said.

"None prettier."

"She cooks, too, all alone in that house. Why doesn't she marry?"

McPherson recognized this as no more than he deserved. "Well now," he coughed. "Marriage isn't for everyone. Maybe she doesn't want a lunk of a man coming around and dirtying her house."

Nora was quiet for three blocks, and McPherson began to calm, seeing the conversation over. "I would," she announced.

"Would what?"

"Want the lunk of man around. What's the point, otherwise?"

At that McPherson stopped dead in the street to stare at his daughter, who appeared unimpressed with her own powers of induction. "You, miss," he said, "know a thing or two."

He wanted to run back to Hannah then and there, leave a trail of settling dust, sweep her up in the finest movie-house tradition, her firm waist and bright lips. Her all alone in that house, making honey cakes for a man who came to her stamped with the dirt of the mine and who left before the sun went down. He was dizzy, amazed, stock still in the street. Nora took his arm and began to walk again. "I

hope she remembers about the recipe,'' she said. "I've done everything I can think of, and there's still more coming up in the garden.
Look, there's a robin on the post.''

Sighing, McPherson fell back into step with his chattering daughter, who held his arm lightly and with such pride.

"I don't understand it,'' Hannah said. "A teenage girl, a pretty
thing.''

"She's too smart for the boys here,'' McPherson said.

"I don't doubt it. But still, Mac. Sixteen years old. Doesn't
anyone call her?''

"How'm I to know? I'm at meetings every night—maybe she's
having boys over. Maybe she's entertaining her whole class.'' He
knew better. When he came in the door at night he could see her
blossom. She listened carefully as he explained about the troubles,
she asked questions and gave him logical, intelligent comments.
"Intelligent! About the damn union! We should have *her* dealing
with the company,'' he said.

The troubles had started when a section of the southern end of the
mine had collapsed, taking eight men with it. McPherson had been
called in to listen while a company man read a statement. The
accident was the result of mining carelessly, too near the supports,
the man read. McPherson didn't know he was even listening. He'd
been quiet in the hall, thinking of the men—Fogarty, Adams—now
buried. He'd been as surprised as anyone when he reared up in the
middle of the statement and cried, "How do you know?'' The
representative had lowered the page he was reading from and glared
at him, but it was too late. McPherson climbed on top of his chair.
"How do you *know?* It only went down five hours ago. Just what are
you trying to sell us?''

That was the beginning. Perhaps if McPherson had been able to
keep still everything would have stayed calm. The company would
have closed off the southern section—as they were planning to do,
and would have told the men if they'd only remained quiet long
enough to hear—the few necessary layoffs would have been made,
and worker safety would have been maintained. As it was, there was
a riot there in the middle of the day, the men screaming, throwing

chairs and the company podium through the windows. McPherson found himself collaring the district manager, shouting, "You sold us our houses, you sell us our liquor and our laundry detergent. What are you selling us now?" He didn't know he had it in him.

When he came home that night it was late. One of his shirtsleeves had been ripped clean away, the small of his back ached from where he'd been kicked or hit, and spidery cuts were etched across his arm; he'd had to jump out one of the broken windows to avoid the police. Nora came streaming out the door to him, laughing, crying. She flung herself into his arms.

"They wouldn't tell me, the bastards," she cried. "Twenty men dead and you not home and they wouldn't tell me anything. 'We cannot give out the information you request. Company policy prohibits—' My God! Twenty men gone!"

"Eight," he said, gently wriggling from her grasp. "Only eight. And me still alive. Come on now, let me wash. I'm too old to be brawling half the day."

She stood by the bathroom door after handing him clean towels; he could feel her trembling presence in the hall outside. "I'm all *right*," he called to her, and then, "Nora, love, fix me some supper, I'm famished." In fact, he had no appetite at all, but whole pots of soup were preferable to emerging, arms stinging and legs weak, to a daughter trembling like a rabbit.

"This means strike, of course," he said over the soup. "God knows how long before we see another paycheck."

Nora sat across from McPherson with her hands folded around a cup of tea; preparing the food had soothed her. "Hays'll extend credit," she said. "He'll have to."

How did she know such things? he wondered. There had never been a strike before. "Let's hope," he said.

McPherson hated the strike. He'd never been one for missing work, and he felt clumsy and trapped inside days with no set pattern. He tried to clean the house while Nora was off at school, but he didn't know what half of her pastes and solutions were. The day he cleaned the kitchen floor she laughed at him for going through half a bottle of polish. "We'll never get through the strike this way," she said, chasing him away from the cupboard.

He spent his afternoons with Hannah, but he left at four-thirty as he always had. He was uncomfortably aware that he didn't know how she spent the billowing hours they weren't together, and it annoyed him that she was so cheerful when he prepared to leave. "We could be taking advantage of this time," he told her. "We could make hay while the sun shines."

She smiled then, hummed a little air. She dusted the headboard with a corner of the pillowcase.

"Dammit, we could be talking to each other. Finding things out. We'll regret it later, how we wasted this time. What do we know about each other?" He crossed the bedroom to her dresser and picked up a photograph that stood near her brushes. "Who's this?"

"Mac, that's my mother. You know that."

"Well, tell me about her. I don't know anything other than her damned cabbage soup. Your own mother."

"What's to say? You knew her. She had a temper. She taught me the things that mothers teach their girls."

"What? What do mothers teach their girls? Tell me."

"Cleaning, Mac," she sighed. "Washing curtains every month. Floors every week. You get the old polish smell out with two teaspoons of vinegar in a bucket of water."

"You know that isn't what I meant."

"Always check to make sure a chicken is fresh," she said, "butchers'll lie. The skin should be butter yellow and firm. Don't ever buy under three pounds, it'll be all bone. Use the feet to make better soup." McPherson was pacing and grumbling.

"Never hang trousers on the line by the waist, it makes them sag. Only use white pillowcases and hankies, and always press them. Have nothing to do with a man whose hankies aren't pressed."

"That's what she taught you?"

"Who remembers? Maybe she taught me to tie my shoes. Maybe she taught me to smile at the men—though I doubt it, that woman. What are you teaching Nora?"

"That's what's worrying me," he said.

At home in the long evenings he and Nora watched each other. He began to test her. "Did you put the feet in this soup?" he asked over dinner.

"Of course. Makes the stock richer."

Or, on walks, he'd point. "Look—Henry must be helping with the wash. Look at how those pants are hung out."

"Few more times, they'll be ruined. Waists'll sag right down to the pockets," she said. He couldn't get over it. Anne could never have taught her so much. How could Nora have learned it all, without him ever knowing?

The work she brought home nights was no less mysterious. Economics, trigonometry—"Shouldn't you be studying with your friends?" he asked.

"They don't know it any better than I do. And if they did, why should they tell me?"

He could hear Hannah laughing. "Will you do well?" he asked.

"I'll do well enough." She did better than well enough, they both knew it. She brought home *A*'s, left them by his placemat to see while the soup cooled. So while neither said it, they both knew: *Well enough to go away.*

"I suppose," McPherson said with great casualness, "we'll need to be thinking about your future." Since the strike he'd seen them coming in, the catalogues and pamphlets from universities. He left them by her chair and she never said anything. She brought them to her room and he didn't see them again. He'd learned to leaf through them quickly before she came home, noting the pictures of pretty coeds with test tubes and musical instruments.

"No need for that now, Dad." And while he knew he couldn't ask for such sacrifices, that he hadn't the right, he could see no harm in keeping her just until the strike was over, until he was back his own man again. Only that, he promised himself as he buried under coffee grounds the catalog from the college in California, where Anne lived.

In his restlessness he was seeing more now than he ever had. When she put her hair up in the morning it stayed perfectly in place until he kissed her good-night. She smelled at any hour of soap and, vaguely, yeast. She never cooked without an apron, she washed her aprons twice a week, but he never saw them soiled. Not even a dash of flour. It worried him.

"Daughter, we're getting dull. Let's go to a movie."

"How can we go to a movie? We could go for a walk. Maybe we'll see Miss Crawley."

He had been sitting in the same place when Anne told him everything she knew about Hannah, when she had systematically spattered the wall behind him with the contents of the refrigerator. He closed his eyes, remembering, and waited for the bottles and jars to crash around him again, but when he looked up Nora's face was as untroubled as milk. She bent to wipe the table, then took off her apron, and they walked together through the twilight.

He found himself watching her simplest gestures, staring, fascinated and appalled by this life with no wasted motion, no excesses.

"Why're you wearing that old shirt? You've got prettier clothes than that."

"Muriatic acid today in chemistry," she said, stirring the oatmeal. And what chilled McPherson wasn't his daughter in a laboratory with muriatic acid, it was the absolute precision of a life that had a good reason, at age sixteen, to wear an old shirt of her father's to school. "Can you take another week of pork stew? Hays says pork'll be down next Tuesday if I can get in before school. Maybe I can coax a few more tomatoes out too, and we can do it right."

"Why don't you have a *boyfriend?*" McPherson demanded, slapping the table so hard his coffee jumped.

She turned then to stare at him. He couldn't for the life of him explain why he'd said it, it was the last thing he could have meant to say. He meant something entirely different, he meant *Why is your hair always tidy? Why do you never break anything? Why can't I guess what you're thinking?* The oatmeal bubbled in the pot. "Do you have anyone particular in mind?" she said finally.

"You're here all the damn time. Cleansers. Soups. Damn ham hocks from the grocer. Every morning you slip in for his rotten bargains. You're sixteen years old, girl. Get out of the house."

"And what should I do then? Go down to the Cue and wait for someone to buy me drinks? Go to the station and hope for a sailor?"

"Nora. Don't be silly, girl."

"Well, you're right, aren't you? Get me a silk blouse, a black skirt. Get me high heels. After all. Can't have a boyfriend for wishing it."

"Nora."

"What do you think? You think this is choice?"

Her face was bleak, blasted—for a moment, it was the face of a woman much older. *Sixteen years old.* What had he done? "Nora," he said helplessly. She stared through him. His own girl, with her creamy face and dark hair. Supple hands, like her mother's. "Hey, Nora-nor," he pleaded.

She came over to him then, rested her fingers on his shoulder. Her mouth was soft and quivering. "What's there here, after all, in this town? Miners and married men. Can't find a beau I like better than you."

Her eyes were round, bright with liquid, and they rested on him so that for a moment he had to catch his breath. "There's never," he said, "been a girl like you."

"Oh, there are plenty like me."

"Not these days. Those college boys will never know what hit them."

"Who says I'm going to college?" She blinked and it was again the catch at his heart but before he could manage a response she went on, "I couldn't live with myself, knowing you were alone in this house." She bent and kissed his head lightly and for a moment McPherson was quite sure that if she ever left him he would die.

"She's in a laboratory with muriatic acid but she says she's not going on," he said to Hannah. "Colleges in California send her catalogues."

"So aren't you happy?"

"Don't be a fool, woman. The girl's brilliant." He knew what happened to the ones who stayed, none better. Hadn't he seen them, all his life? "What's she going to do here? Take a job checking groceries at Hays's?"

"Take care of the father she adores?" Hannah's face was expressionless. He glared at her.

"This strike'll be over soon. The union says another month. Hannah, this is serious."

"I am serious. She can go back to getting the coal dust out of your boxers. What do you want out of the girl? You've convinced her you can't live without her."

"I can't."

"Well, then." She turned over, so McPherson saw only the back of her neck. "She's made you the happiest of men."

"I can't talk to you if you won't look at me."

"I don't see that you need to talk. You're upset she might be leaving, and you're upset when she promises she'll stay. No wonder Anne threw things."

"Don't bring her into it."

Hannah was still for a minute, then said, "Just what do you imagine you'd do with yourself if Nora left?"

"I'd get along. Come home nights, have a drink. Go down to the Cue for a few games."

"You've never shot pool in your life."

"That's not the point. I'd adjust. Get used to a quiet life."

"Well then."

"Well then what?"

"If that's how you see your options."

He looked at the back of her neck, how the lightly freckled skin sloped over her shoulders. He touched her hair. "Hannah. I didn't mean that. You won't be left untended."

"Mac, I'm forty-two. And I'm already untended."

He had the sense then to draw her close, although she lay beside him ungiving as stone. He watched the light play over the long spill of her back and hips. Her skin was warm, as smooth and fragrant as honey. How long had she imagined? McPherson wished he could explain to her. Nora could go to college, to Timbuktu. He would somehow learn, and keep her house for her—her house now, with her solvents, faint soap and yeast. Her own house, after all.

He held Hannah until finally she relaxed and slept and the thick afternoon light diminished. He gently kissed as much of her as he could reach without loosening his hold. It was as close to arguing as they'd ever come. If he held her, if he didn't slacken his hold, they might walk away with dignity, nothing shattered in their wake.

It wasn't until the afternoon was quite gone that he rose from the bed and quietly dressed. Nora would surely be concerned, imagining fantastic things, and he would need to calm her. Not tonight, but soon they would have to begin talking about her going away. Once he helped her see the pride of a solitary life, one lived with dignity and stillness, once he helped her see him in it, she would go. It was carrying on her own tradition, after all—the things she'd taught him. He would practice while she was at school, to find the words.

He walked quickly, cutting up the alley behind his street as he rarely did—it was narrow and foul, and dogs were often there. There was no light, and as a result, he scarcely recognized Nora when he saw her at the corner—recognized really only her posture, the small squared shoulders in the too-large shirt. Not in the kitchen at all, but pressed against the wall of this damp alley, as if waiting. She was standing in the dark, peering into the lit street that led into town. The only house there belonged to Hays.

McPherson stopped and watched his daughter while she leaned further into the light and looked at the house. He could see her face. And had he not been watching, he would have passed her on the street. Stamped across the even features that had come from her mother and the tilted eyes that were her father's own. Gazing at Hays' house. It was wildness, despair. His own daughter.

Hays was forty if he was a day. His wife, his children. His courtesy, McPherson remembered. His small, pleasant comments, his ability to remember relations and birthdays. And then: His cologne. His black hair and well-tended hands. Nora, oh Nora Nora.

McPherson turned as quietly as he could and crept back down the alley, leaving behind him his daughter's wild face. They would meet in the kitchen, and somehow he would have to gather himself, find all the wisdom he had ever known. How else could he help her see? Pain's solace, the only comfort he had been able to learn, was the terrible promise that grief always ends. He began to set the table, thinking that it would be good to have dinner waiting for her when she returned.

Testimonial

My high school class is dying of suicides. For years this was a latent tendency. We didn't construct papier-mâché pill bottles or gigantic razor blades for our senior float; like any silent, internal disease, like my mother's cancer, the symptoms didn't develop until later. Certainly we all thought we were normal—*are* normal—and we've gone the expected rounds; people have attended college, have married, have begun families. Have killed themselves.

It's not something we talk about. I would like to suggest that we're showing new solidarity with the Swedes, who believe in neutrality and commit suicide in great numbers. Or the beginning of a cult phenomenon; there will be pictures of our town in *Time* and psychologists called in to explain. Certainly none of us can. All that's clear is that things are dizzy, sped up, and we're going down too fast, like lemmings elbowing their way to the brink. Every time I tell my mother she ruffles, squawks, refuses to let her tiny black eyes meet mine. She behaves every time as if it were unique, as if I weren't attending funerals as regularly as a season ticket holder. She forgets them, cancels and excuses them, leaves me to keep track. It's eight now.

"There are ways," my mother says, "of looking at everything. You always look for the worst. The worst possible."

She says this because I was the one to tell her what had happened to Kevin. She came into my room later, her voice shrill and ugly, breaking on high syllables. "He was shot down," she said. "His plane was *shot down*. How could you have told me that he killed himself?"

I didn't, in fact. I told her that he took his life, simple truth.
Volunteering, knowing it was dangerous. Knowing he could have
stayed in the camp and protected himself. Knowing he could still
have come back home, he went ahead and strapped himself into that
slick, tight cockpit. It was perfectly clear; how could my mother not
see something so clear? I cried at the ceremony, looking at the folds
of the flag over the empty coffin, and she glared at me as if I had no
right to grieve.

I grieve for them all, every day. Kevin who sent me a postcard
from Saigon that arrived, smudged and torn, a month after his
funeral. Marsha who brought a silver poodle to school with her once
when we were in third grade; the dog wouldn't lie down all day and
clicked around the edge of the room on its arched toenails.

"That girl was sick," my mother says firmly. "Disturbed." She
has to admit this much: Marsha swallowed lye, then dragged herself
through every room in the house, raking at baseboards and upholstery with her fingernails, leaving long, long scratches I couldn't
help seeing at the reception after the funeral was over. But I forget
that, remembering the delicate scrape of the poodle's toenails on the
classroom floor.

It's getting harder. When I first find out, when the telephone rings
and someone tells me, *I knew you would want to know,* it's more and
more often now a scramble to remember, to reconstruct the face and
resurrect the memory that I know belonged only to Marsha or to
Kevin—a poodle, a postcard. It wasn't hard like this at first. Memories then came washing through in a flood I couldn't channel or
control: When Andy Cardiff shot himself six months after we finished high school, I remembered everything I had ever said to him,
the part in his hair, his wide back as he worked algebra problems on
the board. All my mother said was that it was terribly sad, really a
tragic gesture on his part. But we all—no one had had time to go
away yet—*remembered,* that's the point, and we sat the night re-
calling and replaying.

Soon enough, though, people began to leave and marry, and by
the time Miles walked into the lake with rocks in his pockets and
hands the class was already coming apart like fabric. My mother
knew by then about the cancer, how it had fed on her for months, so

for her there was no time or strength to sit with me and talk about Miles. I had to remember alone the times he took me swimming and laughed at the barbershop stripes on my bathing suit. "Don't you remember?" I asked her, wishing she would; I was just learning how hard it is to remember by yourself. She looked up at me with hooded eyes and I left the room before she could tell me that she had other things to remember. My mother and I were locked together like old people in a sour marriage, and I knew her responses before I knew my own questions.

She was dwindling as my class diminished, but it wasn't dependable, her sickness. At first I scarcely let her out of my sight, imagined I could sit and watch as she departed this world; I saw every breath as tenuous, miraculous, her last. Healers came when she could no longer sit up through even the short service, and the sound of their quiet prayers seeped out from under her bedroom door. Pamphlets began arriving regularly from Boston—*Did the healers put her on mailing lists,* I wondered, *or does the mother church just know?* Then she got better.

Color returned to her flesh, she focused on me when we were in a room together with a self-satisfied look that drove me crazy. "It is *not*," I would tell her after we'd been silent together for half an hour. "I know what you're thinking, but you're wrong. These things have remissions, you know. They haven't done a thing for you. Go to a hospital."

"I hardly think you're in a position to tell me what to do," she would say, turning so that the afternoon sun would light her crest of hair, reaching for a pamphlet or the *Monitor.* Now that she was better, she was sending off checks as the pamphlets came in, and we received more of them every day, Mary Baker Eddy's plain face on the second or third page, entreating. "You are dearly loved," it would say under that face in bold script. "You are God's own dear child."

Meanwhile, my class was dropping around me—Judy Wollerman swallowed a bottleful of Valium, Joey Morton drove into the power line along the old state road and blacked out half the county for the night. "That was an accident," my mother snapped, but we all knew better. Joey was the best driver in the class, he was a salesman, driving was his *job*. It was at Joey's funeral that Marlis came up to me and clawed at my elbow.

"We've got to do something," she said. "We've got to stop this. How many can we stand? Six in two years—what's happening to us? Six," she let her voice drop to conspirator's level, "is too many."

I handed her a glass of punch.

"I get so afraid," she said. "Aren't you afraid? I wonder—God help me—I wonder who'll be next."

I held out the cookies for her to take some. *There's no percentage in this,* I was thinking. She looked glassily at the tray and kept talking.

"I sit up nights. Just sit with the blanket around me, and look around the house at all the ways I could do it. There are a hundred things in a bathroom alone. Just there."

"Well, of course," I said, and she finally focused on me, her hands clutching again. "Naturally. You didn't see those things before?"

I had made her cry. Her mouth became thick and shapeless and the tears ran heavily down onto her dress. "I'm afraid," she said again softly. But we were all afraid. Seeing each other at the grocery or hardware store, we didn't meet each other's eyes. We rushed home and watched ourselves maneuver around the iron, the fusebox, the car, lawnmower, electric razor. We telephoned each other to take inventory. "Just wanted to say hi!" we lied brightly. Marlis had cornered no market on fear. Two weeks later, when she tried to slit her wrists, she botched the job and came back from the hospital chastened and scarred. It seemed as if to make up for her that Mark Norris jumped from the National Indemnity building.

"It's tragic," clucked my mother.

"That's seven," I said. "It's getting to be a career option."

"Get out of here," she said, her head darting back and forth. "I won't listen to this from you."

I know she was thinking that I didn't care, but she was wrong. *Mark, oh Mark, you had curly hair that I dreamed of touching, I used to try to get right behind you in the lunch line so that I could smell your clean scent. If I try I can remember it still, being jostled up against your shirt, wishing someone else would push me. I could have spent an eternity leaning against your cotton shirt.*

I went again and again to stand across the street from the National Indemnity building, watched them build a guard rail around the roof. The street crews scrubbed and scrubbed, but the stain on the pavement remained; people skirted it on their way to the bank. I dreamed of Mark in flight or diving, his arms flung out proudly, his legs straight and his toes pointed. How could she think I didn't care?

But she was going down again. The healers were scuttling back into the house and she had begun to sit very still, an hour or more without even twitching.

"I'm praying," she said. "It eases me."

"Go to the doctor," I said. "That would ease you."

She smiled a little, closed her eyes, shook her head. After several minutes she said, "Ease comes in not fighting His will. Why don't you know that much by now?"

There were so many answers. When I was a child, she had taken me to the doctor, His will or not. This, what she was doing, was no ease, it was surrender. Not even surrender, it was volunteering. I left her perfectly still in the wing chair, flanked by pamphlets: *You are God's own dear child. You are dearly loved.* When the healers came back I sneered at them.

This time, under their hands, nothing happened. I stayed in the house in the heat, baking cookies that I wound up leaving out for them—who else would eat them?—waiting for the healers to do it again, waiting for my mother to walk out of her room on her own legs, thin now as bird's legs. She wasted. When I came into her room in the mornings her hands were clenching the sheet; even with my poor vision I could see from the doorway how the veins hunched across her hands. She was so thin I could have carried her in my arms to the hospital, presented her there like long-stemmed roses. I started bringing the cookies into her room when the healers were there, smiling sneakily, catching whatever they let slip as I barged in and repeating it furiously in my own room through all the nights: The Lord is King. Your will be done. Love and love and love. I could no more save her than fly, but I had dreams of catching her up and sailing powerfully above and away.

Then the morning came that her hands were calm, and my first thought—anyone would have thought the same—was that I had lost her. I would call the healers and tell them what I thought of them. I had her water glass in my hand and it wasn't until I set it on her dresser that I saw her light breaths, vowed to make oatmeal-raisin cookies—*They always go the fastest*—and bent to kiss my mother's forehead. Even that was thinner, it was like kissing the skull itself, her skin no more protection than the finest glass. When she smiled at me I expected her to shatter.

The healers came that morning and I showed them with great ceremony into the living room, where my mother was carefully perched on the wing chair. They settled down for restrained hosannahs and smiled at me when I brought in the cookies, and I was willing, God knows, to give them credit for this, Lazarus in our midst, my mother sitting up among them. Now I wished they would hurry up and clear out. I had big plans, had already bought eggs for the custards and rice for the puddings. Now that she'd been brought back, I was ready, agitated, straining to make my mother *look* alive. It made me nervous to see her like that, thin as needles and string. To know she was alive while she was so thin required by itself an act of faith.

So I shooed the healers as soon as I decently could and began to cook. I made soft foods, creamy ones. Food to lap at like a cat. "See if you can't eat all of this, Mother. It will help you get strong." "Look what I made for you, Mother." "You'll feel better when you finish this. You'll have the strength of ten." Ten heartbreakingly thin people. She scarcely spoke, but she ate every meal I gave her, every morsel, and didn't gain an ounce.

She was a medical miracle. It was not as if I were giving her fish and leafy greens; three and four times a day she was putting back soup bowls full of caramel cream, pudding, oatmeal, stew. I began to give her ice cream as a snack, snuck extra eggs into the custards, began to comb old cookbooks for recipes that called for flour and butter in lavish amounts. And every morning she awoke ethereal, the weight of the sheet alone—I was sure of it—keeping her pinned to the mattress.

"So much cooking," my mother marveled. "How can you do so much cooking?"

"It keeps me off the streets," I told her. The truth, of course, was that I liked it, thinking no further than the next menu, the next dozen eggs, going early to the grocery store to avoid crowds. It was like living inside a cocoon. We kept the curtains closed over windows that looked out on the street and backlit our rooms with the western sun that came over the garden.

The phone rang while I was working on a butterscotch pudding, and when I heard Marlis's voice I thought, *I've got to keep her from saying it, I can't stand it.* "My mother," I said brightly, "is much better."

"I'm glad to hear it. Louise—"

"She's eating like a horse. I'm in the kitchen all the time trying to keep up with her. That's what I'm doing now."

"Well, I hate to interrupt you. But—"

"Do you have a good recipe for pound cake? I have all these eggs here."

"*Beth Rigo was found stabbed.* I thought you would want to know." While she waited I kept beating the yolks. They need to be lemon-colored. "Louise?" Beat, beat, beat. She knew I was there; she had to hear the sound of the wisk against the bowl. "The service will be Friday. I'll pick you up, if you want. Louise, are you all right?" Beat, beat, beat.

"I'm fine." *It wasn't me they found, cut and dried.* "I look good in black."

"They found her near her apartment. They say she should have known better than to be out walking there alone. They said it was asking for trouble."

"Well, then." *Ask and ye shall receive.*

"But it wasn't like Beth to take chances."

"No." The yolks were going from lemon to white and I beat them like fury, my aching wrist a blur. I could hardly tell Marlis that I couldn't remember any Beth in our class, but I was sure she wouldn't have been a risk-taker: There are no daredevils named Beth. I would go to find my annual if Marlis ever stopped talking, look at her picture and bone up on her clubs, her goals, see if she hadn't written something over her picture: Never forget Mrs.

Wilson's chemistry course. I would go to the funeral and no one would know that I had forgotten, couldn't remember knowing any Beths.

Maybe Marlis wasn't letting on. Maybe she had forgotten her too, maybe we all had, and the town that night would be loud with the rustle of 1971 *Lamplighters* being pulled out and opened to the *R*s. We would remember her now, by golly. Remember her daily. That's what suicide gets you.

When I brought my mother the pudding I told her that a girl from my class had been murdered. Thin or not, she shot me a look.

"Isn't that sad," she said.

"Eat your pudding."

"Give the dead their due."

"I will. But you like pudding better when it's warm."

She picked up her spoon and began to trace wide trails through the butterscotch. Lately she'd been sculpting her food before she ate it, drawing faces in the oatmeal, spelling out names with crusts—once, her great triumph, building a pyramid of peas. "It's terrible that all your friends are dying so young," she said abruptly.

"It's the choice of a new generation."

"Impertinence is not becoming in a young lady." We watched her spoon's slow progress. "I lost half of the boys I ever dated in high school to the war, but that was different. There was glory then. Do you and your friends know anything about glory?"

"It goes under a different name these days." If she asked me what it was, I couldn't hope to tell her.

"I can't imagine how I would have felt at your age, to have lost so many to just—life."

"Mom." I made my voice as gentle as I could, and it came out husky. I sounded like Lauren Bacall. "Please try to eat."

"Do you understand what's happening to them all? Have you made sense of it?"

"No," I said, thinking, *Make sense? It's all I can do to keep track,* and it was then that she looked up at me and relief washed over her sharpened features, and I wondered how long she had been hesitating with this, pecking at words, trying to find a way to ask me. She shouldn't have had to ask. My own mother, she was the one

who had taught me to know my place, keep to it, and it was clear by
now that my place wasn't among the dazzlers. It wasn't for me to
take headers from ten stories up or court trouble on dark city streets.
Anyone could see that I was a keeper. I was the home front, the
living testimony, the one they died for. "I'm too busy outliving my
mother," I told her, taking the spoon from her hand and lifting the
pudding firmly to her mouth. Other days she wouldn't submit to
this, but this time she laid back and gave me a sweet smile. I could
trace the pudding's progress down her throat by the working of her
muscles. "How do you feel, Mama?"

"Good. Tired. Good and tired."

"Is the pain gone?"

"Oh no, there's still pain. The pain's never gone. We've become
quite intimate."

*She should go to a hospital. She must go right away. Things can
be done. Treatments. Remissions.* Her hair would all fall out. I would
be able to find her anywhere, following the trail of her hair. I kept
spooning the soft pudding into her mouth, thinking of rice soup for
dinner, something she could keep down. When she died, the first
person I would call would be Marlis, knowing as I did that she
would want to know. I would arrange now for a funeral, find for her
music that had angels, the sound of powerful wings. I would order
a headstone, something mammoth, a monument for all the world.
You, it would say in letters deep and large, you have been dearly
loved.

for MMW

Life Drawing

Enid had taken to working later and later at the small studio space the college allotted her. She had learned the names of the two janitors who came to empty the wastepaper baskets, and she noted that the lights over the campus walkways came on later as the days pressed into spring. Sometimes she walked back and forth across the campus for an hour or more before returning to her car and going home. Some nights she graded an entire set of student portfolios. She took great care, commenting on every sketch, trying to work until ten, eleven, twelve o'clock, postponing the time she would have to return home and deal with Melinda.

Enid could see now that when Melinda first came to her, heavy eyes and belly already on the rise, she never should have let her in the door. "But we were *going* to be married," Melinda had said on the front step, chewing her lip, her eyes red. "I *loved* him. He didn't even know about the baby."

Neither did Enid. She had only met Melinda once before, when her brother, Gus, had announced to the family that they were engaged and Enid's single thought had been that the woman looked dirty. Surely, Enid thought then, this had nothing to do with her; it was all Gus's doing, presented like a package, Melinda giggling and swinging his hand in their parents' living room. He had never given Enid anything to help her understand, refused the looks she sent him telling as plainly as she could: *This isn't right. This isn't what you mean to do.* She had never even had a chance to keep him from flying a tiny, fragile airplane into Alaska, a trip he'd said he knew was safe. She couldn't be held now to this slovenly, sniffling woman.

The wedding would have been in two weeks, Melinda said after Enid took her into the kitchen. Now she had nowhere to go.

Enid had known perfectly well what the woman was asking, and so she kept her back turned while she assembled the teapot and cups on a tray. Her parents, she knew, had already told Melinda that they didn't see how they could be expected to help, now, at such a time. Gus was dead and they didn't even have his body—it was legitimate grief that had shut her out. Enid would be foolish to allow her in.

"Gus used to tell me that his family was like a mighty fortress," Melinda said, and blew on her tea. "I didn't know then what he meant. But where else can I go? He told me to quit my job when we decided to get married, I'm pregnant—it isn't my fault. In two more weeks we would have been family, you know."

Enid, who believed in a God she never admitted to, believed that He had made Melinda say that as a reminder to Enid.

"You know that he would have wanted you to help me. You know he would."

Enid went to get bedding for her because she didn't think she could bear another syllable about Gus, and because she didn't want to have to force her out of the house, and because the woman's easy, intimate way of talking about Gus and what he had said and what he would want made her nauseous. She had spent the weeks since the news of the sudden blizzard with her eyes open painfully wide, looking intently at everything that entered her focal plane, sketching with great accuracy cupboard doors and the dashboard of her car. She had taken to listening to radio talk shows, which she detested. She was planting herself firmly in the world, reminding herself that it had not changed. And so she took in Melinda just to make her stop talking about change and loss. Then the floodgates were open.

Enid had never had close contact with a pregnant woman before. While she was able to accustom herself to Melinda's retching every morning and her odd, horrible combinations of food, she was skep-

tical of the daily high drama. "I was sick all day today," Melinda
would greet her when she came home at night, and she sounded
proud of herself. "I think my breasts are beginning to leak. Look."
She would open her blouse for inspection, and Enid would flee.

She was working on a series of miniatures. She had begun them
before Gus's death, and they suited her perfectly now: She lost hours
rounding and shading a single minute orange. She was late for class
so often she finally asked one of the teaching assistants to come and
fetch her five minutes before she was supposed to lecture. She would
get up from the easel tingling at the points of her body—her fingers,
joints. It wasn't precisely exhilaration, there was no great surge of
energy, but rather tiny, contained explosions, like sparklers in her
fingertips.

She had had such perfect concentration since he died. She thought
this only once, and said to herself, "He would be happy to see me
working so hard," although she knew this was absolutely untrue.
He would have folded his long arms and told her to ease up. He
would have smiled and told her that the race is not to the swift. He
would have said that if she was going to paint, she should for God's
sake paint something big enough for a person to see. Upon reflection
she understood that she was working so hard in order to stop thinking about him. That seemed reasonable to her, and she spent a full
weekend coaxing out a single minuscule banana.

When she did come home, late and tired and trailing a faint odor
of turpentine, Melinda would be shockingly there. Enid couldn't accustom herself to it; she still remembered the day she moved into her
own apartment as the beginning of contentment. Even so, it infuri-
ated her that Melinda ignored her when she came in the door, looking instead out a window, her hand brushing lightly over her stomach. It was weeks before Melinda even asked Enid why the brushes
that Enid had brought home to clean were in the kitchen sink.

"What do you paint?"

"Right now, miniatures." Enid was in the kitchen, gathering
plates and silverware to set the table, and stopped to glance at
Melinda. "Small things."

Melinda was standing by the big bay window, doing what Enid's
mother would have called mooning. As the moon rose. Over her

moon of a stomach. She was smiling, too. "I started to be an artist once. That's sort of how Gus and I met. I'm surprised he never told me about you."

"Well." Enid dropped the handful of forks and knives onto the table; sometimes noise stopped her.

"I was the model for his life drawing class. He must have told you that."

"Yes, he must have. Do you want honey with your potatoes again?"

"I always used to model, and I'd tell myself I'd have enough money to buy paint, but most of the time it got spent—rent, sometimes. Dope."

"Do you want honey?"

"I quit modeling when I moved in with Gus, but maybe I should start again now. It would be interesting to draw a pregnant person, don't you think? I'm not so thin anymore."

She turned to Enid to illustrate the possibilities, crouching slowly in her place by the window, then stretching back up onto the balls of her feet, her arms waving like water plants above her head. "You couldn't possibly hold it," Enid said, setting the honey before her plate. "We'll eat in five minutes."

Melinda returned her heels to the ground. "The baby will probably be an artist, don't you think? With all these artists in the gene pool. I'm sure he will."

Later in her own bedroom Enid sketched: the quilt that her grandmother had given her, delicate curtains that shut out not even the faint glow of the streetlight across the road, the pens, jars, handkerchiefs scattered across her bureau. What would Gus have seen to draw in this room? The longing for him rose in her throat, and she drew the jars over and over without ever getting the reflections off the cheap, thick glass. Had he ever drawn shapes, formal things? She wondered if he had done landscapes and portraits, or if all his work had been confined to models in life drawing classes. No matter how hard she looked at what she was drawing, Enid could see him now next to her, on the bed, clear, clear—an easy grin, brown fetlock hanging over his eyes, the length of him—and for a moment she was sure; her hand moved to turn the page. But she had never been able to draw him. He washed off every sketch, slipped like water between fingers and pencil, and while she could visualize him in perfect detail, the drawings were dull and clumsy.

She moved to a chair close to the light switch to get away from him, and focused all of her attention on its faint horizontal shadow. When Melinda came in, she entered without knocking.

"Drawing a light switch?"

"Yes. I'd appreciate it if you knocked before you came into my room."

"Sorry. Can I see your light switch?"

"This is the kind of thing that makes it possible for people to live together. Basic courtesy."

"I forgot. Gus and I, you know, never knocked. Can I see it?" Melinda stood with her hand held out and Enid gave her the sketchpad. Then she watched. She stole moments whenever she could to study the other woman and her enlarging body. It didn't seem possible that anyone could grow so large so quickly. Sometimes Enid thought Melinda would have more than one, just from the size of her—quintuplets, like the Dionnes. Then good-hearted people would start sending gifts and offer her homes. In the meantime Enid had begun drawing pregnant doodles; she liked the sudden curve that erupted from a flat surface.

"That's very good," Melinda said, handing her back the pad. "I'd never think of drawing something like that, but it's very realistic."

"Thank you."

"Maybe I should start drawing again. I have so much spare time on my hands since you're gone all the time."

"Maybe you should." Enid had wondered before this what Melinda had done in her art classes. She imagined sunsets, seascapes, red barns in snowy valleys.

"Could you bring me home a sketchpad? And some pencils, you know. Then I could draw if I got inspired. Make sure you get pencils with erasers on them."

"Anything else?"

"Maybe some charcoal. For shadows, if I see anything like that."

"Yes," said Enid.

"And we could use some groceries. I wish you'd get some fruit."

"Yes," said Enid.

"Apples and bananas. I never used to eat fruit, but I got into the habit with Gus. He ate fruit all the time."

"Yes," she said, picking up her pencil again.

Melinda helped in the house as the spirit moved her. Some days when Enid would return and see Melinda's bloating face in one of the upstairs windows she would prepare herself for the worst, then walk into a house with gleaming baseboards, an antiseptic bathroom. More often there would be a trail of apple cores from the kitchen to Melinda's room, cake and sandwich crumbs on every surface. Melinda would tell her that she had vomited three times that day and Enid would think *No wonder. I would too.* As the weeks passed, Melinda's contributions became more unpredictable—she washed all of Enid's old crystal, legacy from her grandmother. She found the silver, too, and spent three days polishing it. The next day, she brought in the mail.

"Why does your mother write letters to you? She's right here in town."

"I'd appreciate it if you didn't go through my mail."

"It was on top when I brought it in. Why doesn't she just call you?"

Enid and her mother rarely had enough to say to each other to fill a phone call. Their letters were never more than a single page long; her mother would invite her to lunch, Enid would write to accept and then later to thank her. Melinda, she noticed, looked sticky today, as if she had eaten dozens of oranges. Her hair curled up around her face. "My studio doesn't have a phone," Enid told her. "It's easier to reach me this way."

Melinda nodded. "I thought it was kind of funny, because she used to call Gus, you know. All the time. I could tell when it was her because he'd get quieter and quieter, and he'd start drumming his fingers. He wouldn't tell me what she said, but we always went to bed together after she called." She smiled at Enid, who turned her back. She wondered what it would be like to inhabit Melinda's brain for just five minutes. She wondered whether Gus had been

captivated by an inviolable innocence, or if the woman's capacity
for malice was breathtaking.

My dear daughter, the letter began, as always.

*I hope you're managing with your houseguest. If I recall cor-
rectly, her time will come in the early summer. I trust you have
made arrangements.*

*This remains a difficult time for all of us. I am sure you under-
stand why we feel it isn't appropriate to have any lunches now.
Perhaps later, toward August, you will join us? Of course, I hope
you would come to us if you had any needs before then.*

*Your father and I hope that your work is going well. We still look
at and admire the picture you gave us two years ago.*

Your loving Mother.

When Enid looked up, everything was flat. This had happened to
her before, the world becoming two-dimensional, and she could see
precisely how all of it should be drawn, the planes and shadows, the
exact proportions. It was all she was able to see, and she could think
of nothing else; everything around her was translated into pure form.
Melinda stood in front of her and Enid saw cylinders and spheres;
reaching for a pencil was instinctive.

"I did some sketches today," Melinda said, getting to the pencil
first. Enid wanted to cry out, and she almost grabbed for it. "It's
been a long time, but I wasn't as bad as I thought. You want to see?"
She handed Enid a sketchpad that was lying on the table, flipped it
open for her.

Melinda had drawn the view from the big kitchen window—the
dirt path led to the budding chestnut tree and a low hedge—all in
tiny, curving lines. It was recognizable, but stylized. Everything in
Melinda's drawing seemed to float and curve; the branches were
plump and the hedge rounded. Looking at it, all Enid could see was
how it needed to be drawn. She took the pencil from Melinda and
held it firmly, drew as she began to talk.

"Look," she said. "Look. It's obvious what you've drawn, but
you've made it all weightless." She drew over Melinda's faint lines,
made single heavy marks to separate the tree from its background.
"You've got to *look* harder at what you're drawing. You have to see
the form that carries the strength for the whole piece. Once you've

got that, you've got your picture.'' She drew quickly over the sketch, delineating the planes of ground and hedge and new grass, her shadowing hasty and heavy. ''You've got to remember what you're working on. You have to give form to this flat surface—think about *planes* of what you're drawing.'' She turned the page and found a drawing of a bird. ''Same thing here. There are too many useless little lines here. See how much stronger the line is if you straighten this out? You've got to look harder to see what you're doing.'' She was working very fast now, the tingling was beginning again, and when she looked up she had forgotten that it was Melinda standing next to her and not one of her students. ''You see?''

''Is this the way you work?'' she asked Enid. ''On your miniatures?''

''That's a different technique. It calls for a different approach. But this is always at the heart of it.''

''I'm using a different technique,'' said Melinda, taking the sketchpad away from Enid. Enid watched her leave the room, then got her own workbook and began to draw, first birds, then food, finally the backs of women—pregnant, mothering.

Enid made sure there was enough food in the house for several days and brought a cot and a coffeepot to her space at the college; she planned to stay there for the weekend. She tried to explain to Melinda that it had nothing to do with her, simply that the urge was upon her and she could effectively do nothing *except* work, but Melinda left the table before she could finish. By the time Enid got to the studio she had forgotten her.

She tried to work on some of the preliminary drawings for her miniatures, the careful, careful work, but she flipped to clean pages in her workbook; she had new ideas. Figures. She could see the shapes she wanted to get down far more plainly than anything before her in the studio. She drew as fast as she could, but she urgently needed to fill the spaces she saw, give shape to the empty pages that felt as thick as snow, and so she began to paint, washing over pages with watercolor, finally filling big canvases with the widest brush she had. She worked round the clock, testing ideas and wiping them out, molding bodies, joining limbs, running two or three or four together into creatures she couldn't name but whose weight she could feel through her hand. Some of them flew. She filled every surface around her, forms colored like toucans crowding each other on paper and canvas, and all of it only began, all of it only suggested what she was seeing.

By Monday morning she was surrounded by new work, none of it complete, and the brilliance of her vision was gone. When one of her colleagues stopped in to ask what she was working on, she said, "I have no idea." Then she slept until it was time to teach her class, went home groggily and slept again, and so it wasn't until Tuesday morning that she saw Melinda's new drawings.

There were two of them, taped to the refrigerator door. Melinda herself was in her room and her door was closed. The drawings were harsh, filled with brittle lines, and large—they filled the pages and spilled over. They were drawings of Enid. The first was a sketch of her body, arms stretched down to her ankles, body upright like a telephone pole. No waist, no breasts, just a single vertical rod surmounted by a dot of a head—but her, no question. She recognized her own long bones, her old skirt and sweater. The other drawing was a portrait of her face, accurate in every detail: small eyes, long jaw, hair beginning to gray. The face was scored with heavy lines, and the mouth was small and hard as a bullet. In each of the drawings she looked like a witch, and she looked old.

They were like a child's drawings, that direct and impatient. What could possibly have possessed Gus to want to marry such a child? She was suddenly irritated with him. Was this intended for her? she wondered. For the whole family?

Dear Mother, she wrote.

Thanks for your interest. We're getting along here I think just as well as you would have expected—in fact, even you might be surprised. I'm sure this is an object lesson. I'm trying to understand what I'm learning.

She says she dreams of Gus every night. Her dreams, then, seem to be spilling over—I see him smiling in mine every night. Is that how you see him too? Did you think he was smiling when you telephoned him all the time?

I've lived with her now for three months. I've begun to spend all my time in the studio space. I've begun to wonder if maybe he did know, after all, about that storm warning.

She did not, of course, send it.

Enid left the drawings on the refrigerator, not knowing what else to do. She and Melinda didn't refer to them. Melinda was scarcely talking at all; pregnancy was absorbing her, enclosing her, and lately she started at the intrusion of any sound. The intrusions of Enid— the fact that Enid was an intrusion—went without saying. There was no conversation. Enid guessed at what Melinda would want at the grocery store, kept the house stocked with new melons and peaches.

Periodically, perhaps once a week, Enid was greeted by new drawings when she came home. They were always of her, they always relied on a few heavy lines and a thicket of brittle cross-hatchings, but they were never again as violent as the original sketches on the refrigerator. Most of them showed Enid in action— cooking, driving, again and again drawing. Enid studied them. She had never been anyone's model before, and she was disconcerted and fascinated by Melinda's drawings of the straight lines of her body and face. And the drawings were improving. It was true—once you show them how to see, you've done all you can.

Her own work was not going well. Surrounded by the outcome of her frenzied weekend, she was dissatisfied with all of it—the fig-ures were lumpish and disproportioned, there was no unity in what she saw. She returned to her still lifes; once they were all finished she would make herself return to the others, the strange creatures and homunculi all over the room. She felt logy and snapped at her students and colleagues; it was just as well that Melinda didn't want to talk to her.

She found herself posing. Or not so much posing as performing— adjusting herself as she waited for elevators, as if an audience were watching her closely, pencils sketching every line of her body. She began to observe the life drawing classes in order to watch the models, seeing how their wrists fell as if weighted, imagining she could see or feel the motes of dust as they fell on their skin. When she had taken life drawing classes as a student Enid had assumed that the models thought about things other than their nakedness and the play of strangers' eyes on their bodies. *But that's not true at all. It's all they think about,* she thought, pulling down her shoulders, straightening her back.

She was finding it harder to keep to her office hours, harder even to stay in the building, and some afternoons she simply left, driving for miles on country roads she had never before followed. She found no calm or bucolic cure in the dense weeds and overhanging trees whose names she didn't know, but the sheer distance she could carry herself, the feel of tires rolling beneath her, was some satisfaction. Occasionally she stopped and sketched, when she saw wide, flat expanses that attracted her; she had lately a longing for openness, for uninhabited space.

One afternoon Enid came home after her drive rather than going back to the college. She saw Melinda looking out the living room window as she drove up, but she had disappeared by the time Enid came indoors. The house was still. Enid went to the kitchen for a glass of water and saw that Melinda had been there; all over the table there were drawings in untidy stacks. She glanced at the refrigerator and saw that the two original sketches were still there, untouched, then crossed the room to look at the new ones on the table. She stopped there as if struck, suddenly rooted; all of the drawings, dozens of them, were of Gus.

They were obviously all done by Melinda. It was her light pencil and curving lines that shaded the hair and carefully traced the flat shoulder blades, and Enid still felt the irritated desire to strengthen the images, show Melinda what she had meant to do, but it was Gus, Gus; he looked at Enid from every page. There were drawings of him standing against doorframes, sitting at a desk, smiling, always.

Enid was struggling to move, even to breathe. The warm air itself felt palpable, like air in old photographs, and it pressed down on her chest and shoulders until she had to sit down. She picked up the drawings as if they might crumble between her fingertips, seeing the time he had got his hair cut, the shirt he had most liked to wear. She looked at the line of his wrist as he held a coffee cup and thought, *That's right. She got that just right.* She remembered trying to draw that angle, morning after morning at the breakfast table, while her toast cooled and her cereal got soggy. Then she thought of Melinda watching him with a pencil in her hand, her breakfast a banana or an apple, food that would keep while she drew a picture.

Enid got up and closed the kitchen door softly, climbed the stairs on tiptoe; it was not that she wanted to surprise Melinda, but she was caught in the heavy, warm calm of the house. It was like wading through honey. When she came to Melinda's door she knocked as gently as she could. *I want you to tell me about Gus,* she was ready to say when Melinda answered, but there was no answer. She knocked again, even more lightly, knowing already that Melinda wouldn't respond. "I was asleep," she could say later if Enid brought it up. "I have to sleep as much as I can now." Leaving Enid, awake in every fiber, to creep back down the stairs to the pictures.

After that afternoon, Enid forced herself to stay at work or at least to stay on campus, and she continued to observe the life drawing classes. It seemed to her that Melinda was all over the room, in the sulky-looking models and the intense students, and so she began watching the students, too. Most of them sketched with enormous care, their eyes flickering from the model to their sketchpads, and Enid thought she could see Melinda in them, in all of them, but one day she saw a student who simply stared, his pencil loose like a cigarette between his fingers. Enid went to look at what he had drawn. On his paper was no figure at all, just a pattern of heavily shaded planes that opened into white, open space in the center of the page. It was random and beautiful, and the student paid no attention to it, continuing to stare and smile at the model. *Gus,* Enid thought. *Gus.* The memories washed over her then with the force of a wave that has gathered strength over time, from far out at sea.

She remembered him watching things, even when he was tiny, a toddler. She would come into rooms and find him looking out windows with utter stillness. He would turn and smile when he heard her come, but would go back to looking out again without a word. Once when they were alone she came upon him peering into an empty corner of the living room. "What are you doing? There's nothing there."

He gestured to her to come join him. "You can see the air here," he had whispered.

He had liked space, she knew. He made their parents take all of the furniture out of his bedroom, and he slept on the floor, did his homework there—"I want *room* in my room," he told them. When he was old enough to go out by himself, he started to walk long distances, far enough to get away from the houses and mesh of roadways, into fields. He could soon outwalk her, and would come home with clayey dirt on his shoes. When she asked him where he'd been he would laugh, shrug, slip away.

In school he had been bright, precocious—"His insight!" his teachers would say. "His perceptions!" Enid's own teachers would greet her on the first day of school by saying warmly that they had heard of her younger brother. When she walked through the hallways on errands, she had imagined she could hear his laugh from behind the classroom doors.

She brought him things that she thought would please him—candy, sometimes, but more often feathers or rocks or pretty buttons she found—and he took them sweetly from her. He would bring the things he liked best into his room for a few days or a week, and Enid would go out again with wolfish eyes, scouring sidewalks for gifts for him.

Once she started drawing she showed him all her work. She knew he would never comment, but she didn't feel a drawing finished until he had seen it. After Enid had finished her only attempt at a portrait of the family—her mother and father lifelike, Gus as always a little off, thickened—Gus had understood and kept their mother from putting it on the living room wall. "It's what she's doing," he explained to her. "She hasn't done it yet." Enid knew that her mother gave in because Gus had argued for her, not because she understood, but that was all right. After that Enid drew portraits of famous people, faces from the bus: strangers.

When Gus first brought home a girlfriend Enid had only been able to see her in planes and lines, how she divided into light and shade. To this day she could remember the angular feel of her, and how for weeks after that she had only been able to draw things that dropped off sharply, like the collarbones of thin people or steep, sudden cliffs. Of course she had moved away. How could she not have moved away?

Enid leaned back against the cool classroom wall and closed her eyes. He had never even seen her house, she realized. Melinda must have looked up her address in the telephone book. Gus never saw the spacious rooms, the old yard that Melinda watched now from every window. And Enid longed to show it to him—the house, the college, her new work. Even knowing that he didn't want it, that everything she gave him sent him a step further back. Even knowing that he had fled to the space and air of Alaska. Standing, trembling, her shoulders against the wall, Enid understood the storming grief of war widows. She understood the need to have his body—a grave to go to, lie down on and embrace. The need to tell him and no other: You have been loved. Because though he would want to smile and slip away, she would hold him there and force him to feel her, the strength and duration of love, until he was made to bear its weight.

Talk Show

Helen called about voice lessons after she heard herself on the Cary Lucy Show for the first time. She was startled at the sound of her own voice, its flat vowels and the hissing that crackled back to her from her radio. *No wonder,* she thought after she heard it. *This explains a lot.* It was a humiliation to go on radio, over public airwaves with such a voice, so she reached for the Yellow Pages on the bedside table. She took it as given that she would call him again.

She listened to Cary Lucy night after night, lying on her back in bed. She had never listened to call-in radio shows before; she was fascinated with the things people said. "Hello, in response to that last caller? With the noisy dogs next door? I just want to remind her that those dogs are communicating, and dogs are *supposed* to bark. I mean, they're probably happier than she is. I think it's just very selfish asking them to be quiet."

And all Cary Lucy said was, "You've got a good point there." Helen couldn't believe it. She would remind herself that it was his job to be polite and to hear people out, and she imagined how hard it would be to suppress the desire to set these people straight.

After she had listened for a few weeks, she began to pick out the regular callers, and she could anticipate their tirades on race relations, gun control, fluoridation. She settled back as she imagined Cary Lucy himself was doing when the man called in about communists, knowing that he was good for at least five minutes. It would be an ideal time to step out and get a sandwich or go to the bathroom. Maybe Cary Lucy looked forward to these calls. Maybe he played solitaire while they kept talking. He's got to do something, Helen thought. To listen to everyone thoughtfully, patiently, really listen, night after night—he would have to be Christ Himself.

She listened as if addicted, muttering responses impatiently and equally to the anti-Semites, the anarchists, the passionate advocates for animal rights. She didn't hesitate to tell them when they were being arrogant, or partisan, or just blind dumb. "Thick," she'd say to the radio. "Thick as two short planks." But Cary Lucy's program was a solace, distraction during long nights that were blank without him. She had no illness, there was no pain that kept her awake; her body simply shrugged off sleep. It was as if she were old, but Helen knew she wasn't old. Cary Lucy said so himself, often: "Fifty? Why, fifty's not old. Gosh, life *begins* at fifty." She would have liked to call him up then and there and ask him *who, whose* life begins at fifty—certainly no life she knew. But she imagined that he might be right, and she had no desire to call up Cary Lucy only to be rude to him.

Really, at the start she had no desire to call Cary Lucy at all. She just wanted him to keep talking in his soothing voice; she admired his ability to hold his temper through all of the foolish calls, or the surly ones, or the ones that bordered on hysteria. She had read once that programs such as Cary Lucy's have a screening operator to keep the uncontrollable calls, the obviously deranged, off the air. *These are the good ones,* Helen would marvel. And she would listen more carefully, turning up the volume, proud of Cary Lucy's ability to stay serene and polite. When Helen tried to think of kind people, civilized, nice people, she thought of Cary Lucy.

And she felt that she, at least, knew her place as a listener. Wasn't it for her, after all, that these people were talking? What good would the show do, what even would Cary Lucy do, without her?

After discovering the program, Helen listened every night, looking out her window. She watched the clean sheer winter air give way to the heaviness of August, when the lights from Los Angeles turned the night orange. As the weather got hotter she moved out from under the bedclothes a layer at a time until finally she listened lying on top of her sheet in a thin nightie, damp over every inch of her body. Because she had all the windows in the apartment open, the radio had to overcome the gunning engines and laughter and fighting from the street; one night she heard noises she couldn't identify, and in the morning found the walls of the apartment garage spray painted with jagged initials and phrases in Spanish. And Cary Lucy's callers all seemed to Helen to be getting higher pitched, more passionate, even though Cary Lucy's voice stayed steady and calm. *That man,* Helen thought, *has an air conditioner.* And she lay still, concentrating on the voices over the heavy air and the noises from the street. Still, when a caller began talking about self-reliance and survivalism and bomb shelters, it was more than she could take. She dialed Cary Lucy's number quickly, peering at the telephone dial in the dark; she knew the number, of course. After months of listening, she knew the number as well as her own.

She was in a fine fury, rehearsing the phrases to demolish the man's sorry argument—her mind ranged quickly from the Bible to fragments of speeches she remembered from 1972, when Henry Kissinger was making so much sense. "Good evening, this is the Cary Lucy Show," a woman's voice said. "Do you have something you would like to say to Cary Lucy?"

Helen, unprepared for a woman, fumbled. "Yes—well. I do. Not to him, really, but that caller—that is, I have something to say."

"Please hold the line," the woman said. Her voice was lovely— low-pitched and musical. *Peggy,* Helen thought. Cary Lucy mentioned her sometimes, just as he talked about Danny, the show's engineer. "Cary Lucy will take you just as soon as he can; there are two calls ahead of you." Then there was a click and Helen was alone. The caller on now was talking about the city bus problem; it took him two hours just to get downtown to work. Helen could barely remember what she meant to say, the lovely words—*détente, understanding*—and the fury of the moment were gone. She felt as if she were about to go on stage—she, proud to be just a listener, full of restraint. The hand holding the receiver to her ear was sweating. She hung on stubbornly; it would be rude to hang up. It happened sometimes, with some callers, that Cary Lucy would pick up a line with his pleasant, "Hello, you're on the air," only to be greeted with silence. He would always make a graceful little joke and go on to the next caller, but Helen was angered at the insensitivity of people. She hung on.

The next caller was talking. Helen barely listened. Peggy had said there were two calls ahead of her, but still Helen didn't know how soon she would be on the air, talking to Cary Lucy and anyone else who might be listening. She kept trying to put together something to say, to remember what that idiotic man had said. She couldn't imagine now why it had angered her so. She remembered Henry Kissinger saying, "We must work together, to the mutual benefit," and she clung to the words, repeating them over and over. Propped against the pillow, she clenched the receiver, and when she heard "Hello, you're on the air" in her ear and it shot back at her six seconds later from the radio, she started right in.

"Hello, Mr. Lucy."

"Please turn down your radio," he said pleasantly, his voice on the phone overlapping his voice from the speaker, and she was already reaching for the knob, angry with herself for having forgotten. In any case it was too late—she had already heard her voice come back to her, heavy, hissing like a kettle. Again she had lost the thread of her own argument, thinking instead, *I sound like somebody's mother. I sound like my own grandmother.*

"My name is Helen Sawyer," she enunciated carefully.

"Hello, Helen. What do you have to say tonight?"

His s's don't hiss, she thought. *How does he do it?* "In response,"—she winced—"to reply to the caller who was talking just now about self-reliance and being on guard against the Russians, I would just like to remind him that we have no choice except to depend on them, to trust them. In fact, we have an *obligation* to trust them—that's right. Obligation. If we all build bomb shelters the way he said—well, that's the road to tragedy. We have to live together."

Cary Lucy let a moment pass, then said, "Well, thank you, Helen. I'm sure many of our listeners will agree with what you have to say."

"I used to be a nun," Helen said abruptly, and was so horrified with herself that she covered her mouth with her hand, there, in the dark.

"Is that right?" said Cary Lucy.

"I left the order," she told him.

"Well, that's very interesting, Helen. Why did you do that?"

Helen knew she had to say something right away; this was radio. Cary Lucy would worry about dead air. But she had never been given such a question: It was an opportunity. It was lovely, really. "I felt the need," she said very slowly, "to help people directly. It wasn't enough just to worship in the order. I felt that I had to give aid to those in need."

"Well, that's wonderful, Helen. I'm sure this is an inspiration to many of our listeners. What do you do now that you're not a nun?" That voice, smooth as chocolate sauce.

"I work in the community," Helen said hastily. "Community service work."

"Isn't that fine."

"Yes, well. We all do whatever we see fit."

"I certainly hope that's true, Helen. Do you have anything else you want to talk about tonight?"

This was heady, dazzling—after hearing it asked of caller after caller every night for months, Helen suddenly heard the invitation there. "No," she said. "Not tonight." And thinking, *I could have told him anything. Anything at all.*

Helen had never been a nun, exactly. She had entered the Daughters of Mary and Joseph novitiate in 1948, at 18, certain of a vocation that shone like silver in her mind's eye. And after two years there of abstinence and struggle and the glory—*glory*—of her holy life, Helen had been told by everyone, the Mother Superior and her father confessor and eventually the other sisters and the new novices and the cats who slept in the junipers around the convent house that she had no vocation. "How do you *know?*" she had cried at them all, one at a time, all at once, she couldn't remember well anymore. "How do you know?"

She had stayed on with the order for years serving as a lay sister, typing school bulletins and coordinating the paper drive. Finally they had told her that she had no vocation even for that, even for willing service. "It is not," the priest who had been her confessor told her, "that your work is not appreciated. But your spirit is hungry, avaricious—you are not with God."

"Isn't it for me to judge that, Father?"

"It is not," he said. "You must pray for guidance."

Where will I find guidance if you keep pushing me away? she had wanted to cry out. *How can you expect me to pray?* As she remembered it, the priest ended the discussion by sliding shut the door of the confessional, although she knew they had been talking face to face in the convent parlor.

Helen found work with the Department of Motor Vehicles in San Pedro, and she strove every day to be charitable, thinking *This is service.* Later, when she began to think instead *This is penance,* the work became easier.

She lived the way she had learned as a Daughter of Mary and Joseph, plainly, in a small, mean apartment in the Chicano section near the harbor. She was chaste and prayerful, and her civil service job saw to it that she was kept from the ways of wealth. In the years since she left the convent she had kept her life spare and continued to pray six times a day, proud of her discipline, proud that she could carry on even without the bells and plainsong. The introduction of Cary Lucy into her life was sudden softness, like a rich dessert she returned to every night.

Every speech therapist Helen called the next day on her lunch hour asked what sort of therapy she felt she needed. "I would just hate to waste your time, ma'am. I certainly can't hear any abnormalities," one therapist with a young-sounding, supple voice said. For a moment Helen was tempted to say, *You. I want to sound like you,* but she controlled herself. She rarely used the telephone, and to be there, at the pay phone and in full view of all, made her feel vulnerable. Helen was hardly ready to tell these people that she needed to rectify her voice for a late-night radio call-in program, so she worked her way doggedly through the listings until she found a clinic that simply made an appointment for her. "Do you have anything very soon?" she asked. "I get off work at five o'clock."

"We have a five-forty-five on Thursday," the receptionist said.

Helen gave the woman her name and home telephone number. All day, as she corrected driving examinations and adjusted the camera for license photos, she tried to imagine the kinds of exercises they would give her, and practiced pursing her lips, pronouncing her *t*'s and *d*'s with great precision. The muscular young man in an undershirt whose picture she was taking looked at her curiously and smiled, and Helen suddenly realized how she must look, rounding her lips around the hard consonants. The man had to ask her for the receipt, and as he left Helen rushed into the employee bathroom and stayed there as long as she dared.

That night she turned the radio on ten minutes before the show began, to make sure she missed nothing, not even a note of the theme music, and when it did begin she listened harder and heard things she had never heard before. Behind one caller's voice was a faint crackling, as if she were frying bacon while she talked. With another call she heard what sounded like a grocery-store intercom: announcements of in-store specials, requests for price checks. Could someone be calling Cary Lucy from a grocery store? *Of course,* Helen thought. *That must be it.* She was hearing now, after so many months, what Cary Lucy heard. He didn't, after all, do the show to hear people's foolish ideas, to laugh at them—she had always known it. It was to hear what was behind their words, the extraordinary facts of their lives. To fry bacon at midnight, to do the grocery shopping! Their views on anything could never be more interesting than that. Helen leaned closer to the radio, turned up the volume.

"Scandal, is what it is. When I was a girl I could walk anywhere and my parents knew I was safe. There was respect then." Helen, listening for the ringing of cash registers behind the voice, barely noticed what the woman was saying. *To call Cary Lucy like that, in public. Doesn't anyone notice? Don't they see what she's doing?*

"So now there's this new case, and the girl's only thirteen. And nobody's going to do anything about it, and that's a scandal."

"It is terrible," Cary Lucy said.

"It's worse than terrible." Helen thought she could make out a price check on olives. "If it was the mayor's thirteen-year-old they'd get on it quick enough, I'll tell you."

"You may have something there," he said.

"What's that girl supposed to do?" the woman demanded, her voice louder and harsher. "Who's going to make it up to her?"

Helen was already dialing. They would all make it up to her. They could pray for the girl. They could work together, put together a citizens' lobby. If they brought it to the media, county agencies would be forced to take action. *We are not powerless,* Helen practiced. *Not unless we allow ourselves to be.* When Peggy answered Helen was ready, and told her smoothly that she had a response to a call. She turned down her radio, and when Cary Lucy's voice spoke into her ear, she said, "I was raped when I was thirteen, too."

"Do you want to tell us about that?" he asked pleasantly.

She opened her mouth and abruptly closed it again. There was so much she could say. She could talk all night and not say half of it; she felt as if she, a poor swimmer, were bobbing suddenly in a vast, treacherous lake. When she tried to speak she faltered, stammered.

"There, there," Cary Lucy said. "You just say whatever you want. You don't have to go into it if it's too painful."

And she couldn't have been more grateful. She began to talk as if paddling toward his proffered life preserver. "It was so long ago— I'm old now, you know—and I haven't thought about it for—oh, years. It wasn't something we could talk about then, and so my mother told me not to think about it. I spent a long time learning not to think about it, but everybody knew, of course." Outside, the sound of teenagers singing, laughing. A bottle broke.

"Do you think it would have been better if people had been open about it with you?" Cary Lucy asked. "If you could have talked about it?"

"No. I didn't want to talk about it. But maybe if we had moved, so people wouldn't have known. The boys all knew." Helen was horrified to feel tears beginning to well up—even for this, a story not strictly true. She hadn't yet turned thirteen. And it hadn't been rape, precisely; her Uncle Maxwell had touched her, rubbed and caressed her body in ways that no one else had ever done, and that she thought she had by now forgotten. But still, surely, not rape.

"What do you think the parents of this little girl should do?" Cary Lucy asked.

"Leave her alone," said Helen. "They can't take it away from her." She still remembered all of it: He had smelled of bay rum and used to smile at her secretly at dinners and holidays, and her mother always sat between them on the sofa. After her parents found out, Helen never saw him again, never heard his name. "People will only make it worse by talking and talking and talking about it. Believe me, she already knows that everything is different for her now. If they talk to her they'll just ruin everything."

Helen hung up before Cary Lucy could say anything or ask if she had anything else to say. She lay back and thought grimly that the calls would pour in for her now, and the tears ran onto the pillow and pooled in her ears until she could barely hear the radio at all.

"Read this chart," the technician said. "Just speak as you normally do, and make sure you direct your voice toward the microphones."

Before Helen stood four microphones attached to different kinds of machines; one looked like an ordinary tape recorder, another had a needle poised over a long piece of paper, like machines she had seen to chart brain and heart disease.

"Excess," she read carefully. "Perpendicular. Recreation. Permissible. Bob Bently sleeps soundly." The needle was skating wildly over the paper; Helen was nervous watching the thin canyons and steep slopes she was making. *It's exaggerating,* she thought. *It isn't that bad.* But she remembered how she had sounded on her own radio. "Mosquito," she read. "Tempest. Artie Shaw the artisan."

After ten minutes the technician told her to stop, turned off the machines and removed the paper. He picked up a book and handed it to her. "Now just read from this while I watch you." Helen's hands were damp as she opened the book at the marker; the pages stuck to her fingers. His eyes were fastened on her lips and she had to clear her throat twice to find voice enough to read.

" 'The Lord is my shepherd, I shall not want. He makes me lie in green meadows. He leads me to the restful waters; He refreshes my soul. He guides me in the ways of righteousness for His name's sake. Though I pass through the valley of shadow—' Don't you have anything else I can read?" she demanded, looking up to see him writing quickly in a notebook.

"You're doing fine," he said, still writing.

"Something else."

He shrugged, then leaned forward and flipped the book open nearer the front. There the print was larger, and the edges of the page were thin and grimy. "How about this?"

" 'Frank the pelican was the prettiest pelican Susie had ever seen.' " Helen stopped.

"We like to use the same readings, so that the data's consistent."

Helen remembered then all of the children in the waiting room. She had burrowed into a magazine to avoid the dull eyes of the silent ones, and to block out the quick, Spanish conversation of the others. What would those flat and foreign children have to do with pelicans?

" 'His feathers were white all over, and his pouch for scooping up fish was strong and yellow. Sometimes Susie went around the house trying to scoop up whatever she found in a pouch she made in her mouth.

" ' "Oh, Susie," her mother would say. "You're a pretty silly pelican." ' "

"That's fine," said the technician.

By then, Helen was a little sorry to stop. She liked the bounce and sway of the story. She would have liked to take it home with her.

The technician closed his notebook and put his pen back in his pocket. "That's all," he said. "Unless you have something specific you want us to test you for?"

"Well, just—everything." *I want to sound good on the radio.* She could no more have said it than fly.

"We'll have to have these analyzed, so we'll call you in about a week to set up a consultation and therapy." He had already begun to walk toward the door, and Helen wanted to pull him back, to have a chance to watch his mouth working as he explained all of this to her.

"Will there be a lot?"

"Not too much. Not much more than usual. In a few weeks you should be hearing some real results." Helen waited there, looking at the quiet instruments, until another technician came in and showed her out through the waiting room. She had hoped to stay until they were all gone, the Mexican children and the dim ones who would all be struggling with "Frank the Pelican" and psalms while someone carefully watched their mouths.

That night Helen moved her telephone all the way across the room, so that it was almost in the closet. She didn't want to be tempted to call Cary Lucy when the callers started talking about terrorism, morality, corruption at high levels. Listening to Cary Lucy talk, she wondered if he had been born with a voice seamless as oil, or if he too had put in time with nervous needles and waiting rooms full of the stutterers, the dull, the foreign.

The noise from the street was even louder than usual, as if the hot, wet air were pushing the sound down, channeling it into her apartment. Helen turned up the radio twice, but still Cary Lucy was drowned out by throbbing engines and high, hard laughter, and finally she went to the window, not even bothering to put on her robe.

The streetlights had been shot out long before, and Helen couldn't see anything clearly in the dark street. She imagined the teenagers leggy and quick as mosquitoes below her. They were shouting and singing in Spanish, she heard cans and bottles exploding on the street, and they laughed without pause. One of them, she thought, was dancing. In such heat, a person would have to be feverish to dance or even move, to do anything save lie very still, flesh spread out to the air. Maybe, Helen reasoned, it was her own fever that saw them dancing. Maybe too her own fever that caused her to cry out, "Stop!" then, softer, "Please stop," and her overheated imagination to believe she saw them gathering, quieter now, under her window.

"What do you say?"

The voice came from the darkness. If she could only see, Helen thought, it would be easier, and she could control the shaking that began as she bunched the curtains in her hands. "Just—please stop. I need some quiet here." Then for a moment it was entirely quiet and she pleaded, "Don't you need rest? Ever?"

There was rapid conversation in Spanish, and then so many of them laughing, all at once. "No, lady," the voice rose up. "We don't need no rest. You're busy in the day, right? We're busy now. We haven't bothered you yet, right? You better not bother us."

"Or," another voice cut in, dark with laughter, "we'll send you back. Deport you, right? We *let* you stay here, remember that. And we'll send you back. Right?"

Helen tried to talk, but all she could do was work her dry mouth open and shut. They turned up their radio and the brassy music flooded into the street, up the alleys and driveways. "Right?" they called up to her, laughing again. "Right, *gringa?* You got that right?"

Finally she just backed away from the window, her mouth still working, and picked up the telephone. Bent over, half-kneeling with it on the floor of her closet, still shaking, she told Cary Lucy, "I had a baby. They took her away from me," and thought, *This is more true than not.* She had always meant to say it.

"Do you want to talk to us about that?" Cary Lucy asked her.

Helen knew how she must sound. Her dry mouth was quivering so that she could scarcely form words. And she knew that Cary Lucy must be hearing the shouting and singing from under her window— he could hear it all. *He knows everything,* she thought, *everything about me. No one else has ever known so much.* "They said I wasn't fit, and they took her away."

"Why, that's terrible," said Cary Lucy.

"I was a good mother," said Helen.

"I'm sure you were," he said.

"I'll never forgive them." And this was true, true. She had applied for the baby, she knew her birthday, her weight—she had seen her photograph. *She needs a home,* they'd said, and Helen had stepped forward. And it wasn't until later that they explained to her that they meant, *She needs a family,* and then she watched the people with too many children already take the baby with them.

Helen clung to the receiver long after Cary Lucy had hung up, squatting damp next to her shoes, her memories washing over her like heavy water until finally she groped for her radio on the bedside table and went with it into the kitchen. There she sat at the table with her ear next to the speaker. She stayed there all night, fell asleep awkwardly at the table, and when she finally stood to shower and dress in the morning, after the street had been quiet for some hours, it was Cary Lucy's voice that she clung to, to smooth the tremors from her arms and face.

"Your problems are fairly common," the therapist said. "You over-palatalize and so your glottal stops are weak and your fricatives overextended. See this pattern?" She pointed to a series of peaks and valleys on the page on the table before them. "This is descriptive of your pathology."

Helen nodded. She felt weakened with the very idea that her speech had a pathology.

"The therapy isn't hard. If you practice every day you could be speaking fluidly in just a few months." The therapist spoke quickly, and Helen found herself listening for palatalizing and fricatives. She wondered if this woman knew she had made the chart that described her pathology by reading "Frank the Pelican."

"You'll need some things—a portable tape recorder with a microphone, a mirror, a respirator, a regulator for some of the later exercises. And the book, of course. You can get them here, at the receptionist's desk."

Helen nodded again, imagining that the other woman would think she had no voice at all after this interview.

The therapist was busily writing on pieces of paper. She handed Helen a card. "Give this to the receptionist for billing. Make an appointment to see me in about two weeks, and we'll see how you're doing." She smiled briefly. "The exercises will feel awkward at first, but stick with them. Once you get used to them they'll be second nature, and you'll see how much prettier you sound." She swept out of the room.

Prettier? Helen thought, and blushed. It had never occurred to her to sound prettier. *Just smoother, is all. Just so people will listen.*

After she came home with all of her packages, she set them up on the kitchen table, under a strong light, as the receptionist had recommended. "Puh," she said into the microphone. "Puh, puh, puh." She watched her cheeks swell with every inhalation. "Throp. Thlop. Slop. Stop." She went through the first two lessons twice, trying to listen to herself and regulate the flow of air over her palate, but she only vaguely knew where her palate was, and it was impossible to hear or correct herself in the awkward syllables. "Frank the Pelican," she said, feeling the warmth of her breath as she said it. "Frank the Puh-Puh-Pelican." When she played back the tape and listened to herself she heard the same heavy voice she had heard over the radio splaying the words and syllables, and she turned off the machine. It would be time for Cary Lucy soon.

She took a shower and washed her hair. The weatherman on the news had said a cooling front was moving in, but Helen's apartment was still and hot, and the curtains hung limp beside every window.

Helen moved cautiously into her bedroom. For weeks, since the night she had cried out her window, she had not turned on the bedroom light, knowing she was foolish, knowing they all knew just who she was and where to find her. Lately, for the first time in months, Helen felt tired. Not sleepy, but weary, like a swimmer who can't get to the shore. Her back and arms—and now the root of her tongue—ached, and she could feel how close the tears always were. *The heat,* she thought. *It's debilitating. People go crazy with too much heat.* But it wasn't enough, it was no explanation, and lately she was feeling her determination and self-discipline draining away. She should, she knew, have done the voice lesson again. She lay down on top of the bed and turned on the radio.

Cary Lucy's voice was as calm and reassuring as waves, but Helen couldn't concentrate. She kept shifting her position on the sheet, trying to find cool spots. She went into the bathroom and took two aspirin. In the close bedroom, in the narrow strip between her bed and the bureau, she began to pace. The callers were no different—a baby began to cry while one woman was talking, a man complained about taxes and the trilateral commission and Helen listened to his television in the background. A girl called. "I'm fifteen," she said. "I've never done this before."

"Welcome to our show," said Cary Lucy. "Do you have something you want to talk about?"

"Yeah, I do. Or sort of a question. I don't understand why things are the way they are with people. I mean, people call you every night about all kinds of stuff, so obviously they care, but nothing changes. Why is everybody so unhappy?"

"Well, that's a good question," said Cary Lucy.

"I mean, I know it's not that simple, but really, it is, sort of. If everybody's unhappy, why isn't anyone doing anything?"

"That's a very good question. I'm sure our listeners will have a lot to say about that."

Helen kept herself from calling as long as she could. She made herself listen to the tape recording of her voice. She said, "You can't trust yourself." She unplugged the telephone. But Helen was weepy with fatigue and heat, she couldn't fight anymore, *There are things,* she thought, *that need to be said.* While she waited on the line, she didn't practice anything. She had no planned speeches, no quotes or inspiration. When Cary Lucy answered, she said, "I've called you before."

"Well, we're always happy to hear from our frequent listeners."

"I've said some things I didn't mean."

"Is that right?" Cary Lucy sounded a little nonplussed.

"Things have never been easy for me," Helen said.

"The world is a difficult place for all of us."

"I don't know about that," said Helen. "It seems easier for some than others." And then the words came rushing. "It is easy for some. I can see it, I know it. It's smooth. It's easy for you, isn't it?"

"We all have our own problems—" Cary Lucy began.

"What are your problems?" she demanded. "What has ever hurt you?"

"I hardly think—" he said.

"When have you ever lost a baby? When have you ever lost anything?"

"We have all lost—" Helen could hear the little give in his voice, like tiny seams popping. She felt power streaming into her body, and flexed her hand around the receiver.

"What? What have you lost?" She could see him, neatly pressed slacks, perfect teeth. Oh, she could just see him. "What have you ever lost?"

"Look, ma'am, I don't know who you are—"

"What have you lost? Who? Tell me."

There was a long silence, and Helen thought, *I've made him cut me off. He won't listen anymore.* She waited, her mouth dry. She began to silently mouth her palate exercises. When his voice came back, it was pure and lovely. "You're listening," he said, "to the Cary Lucy Show. It's one-thirty-one here in Los Angeles, and our lines are open. Do you have anything else to talk about tonight, ma'am?"

"No," Helen said. Relief was heavy as a weight across her chest. "Not tonight." She lay down then. His voice was liquid, intimate, and she imagined it buoying her up and bearing her away. She listened to the program all night, her eyes comfortably open in the dark.

Finding Sally

Two years passed with no word of Sally. When she left it was as if by tornado, powerful winds that lifted her away while we stood gaping below. After that, everything subsided; day followed day on mere breezes, just enough air to make a banner flutter and snap.

If I'd suspected she might come back I would have waited, I would have lit candles in every window. But it had been two years without word, without *breath* of her. When Anne called to say she had been spotted, I spent five minutes trying to calm my racketing pulse, gazing into the sullen air outside and snapping the desk lock in and out of position. I'd learned to retool. I'd shut doors, and couldn't simply run anymore to the places she called us. I worked for a company that produced movies; there were tall stacks of folders on my desk. Life had grown complex in Sally's absence.

But Sally. Drugs, voices. Everything washed before me as if I'd never put it aside for even a moment, and I called Anne back. "What happened to the warthog?" I asked. This was Sally's husband, a Zen teacher from Nova Scotia with a face bristled and pocked. Next to Sally, whom we called Little Miss Helen of Troy, his ugliness had been breathtaking.

"Who knows?" said Anne. "She's here now. Bring maps with you tonight."

My phone kept ringing after that—agents, writers, people with ideas. It was an hour before I could get another outside line. "Are you sure her mother doesn't know? I don't want to restart it all with her mother."

"This doesn't have anything to do with her mother. We just want to see Sally."

"What if she won't let us?"

"Then we'll knock her out of the way," Anne said sweetly and hung up.

The first time I saw Sally was at the bottom of three flights of stairs. Slumped on the cement, her hair fanned across her back, she was as lovely and defenseless as clouds, so slender that her light dress looked scarcely inhabited. She was a vision, and at that moment, I was certain, stranger as she was: I wanted to save her from whatever had laid her waste, to spring to her defense. Looking at her I felt bold, and larger than life, and a current crackled through me like fire. Her throat, when I clattered down the steps to her, was white, and pliant as a stem.

"I don't know where I am," she whispered as I stood above her.

Her eyes were wide and clear; looking at them was like looking through blue glass, and she watched me with perfect serenity. I could have done anything under the gaze of such clear eyes.

I managed to carry her upstairs, slung across my back, and arranged her on the sofa. Her skin was soft as a child's—despite my care, there were red wheels around her wrists where I'd clung to her. She watched me holding those tender wrists, and I went to get clean soft cloths, my step as swift and sure as my mother's had sounded when I was a child. "You're all right," I told her as I bandaged. For once I knew just what to say. Lines from movies, the words of heroes, caretakers. "You're with me."

We all had stories like this. Anne found her one night at a bus station, helplessly standing before the schedule and weeping. When Anne asked what was wrong, she said, "There is no bus to Paris." And she lifted up her face to the schedule as if she had simply missed it, the 8 P.M. limited from Los Angeles, and Anne, that hard woman, said, "Have you had any dinner? Here, let me buy you something to eat."

It was not that Sally couldn't be trusted. It was the world we couldn't trust with her. We met, the group of us, as we hastened to rescue her from pawnshops or crisis intervention centers. We rec-

ognized each other. The image of her was clear in our eyes and in the
ways our hands reached out, clear as anything secret and binding:
Masonic handshakes, messages sent in code. United by the silky
urgency of her need, we crouched over telephones and lurked near
newsstands. I cut back my hours at work, Martin quit his job entirely and moved back home with his parents. We charged over
highways for her, sacrificed sleep, meals. We rendered her our perfect devotion. In return, she showed us the world.

There was no place she wouldn't go, no place she had sense
enough to stay out of. She took the hands of perfect strangers, who
saw her transparent eyes and told her how they yearned to make her
happy. We wrenched her out of psychotherapy, Young Republicans,
a coven; found her at gay festivals and shooting galleries. We had
seen her slam her long, perfect body into walls and doorjambs after
swallowing pills that someone slipped into her hand. A warty husband and all the lox she could eat were *tame*.

And no one had ever needed any of us so much. "Oh, thank you,"
she said when we brought her back, time and again.

Sometimes we didn't even need to bring her back. People came to
her; one night I returned home and found her sitting beside my door,
happily listening to a young man in a suit who stroked her hand and
talked about the gateways to her deepest self. I ran him off with a
fire ax and fiercely slept that night on the sofa, with Sally in my bed.
It was what I fought for. To save her, to capture back that bright
beauty, to return her to our upright world where we could see her,
day by day.

Holding my head at my desk, imagining her breathy voice asking
someone to help her, I remembered the old longing. It rose up fresh
and whole as desire, and I reached for the telephone to dial her
mother's number.

"Don't think anything has changed," her mother answered the
phone. "Nothing has changed."

"Is she all right?"

"She has nothing to do with you."

"How is her health?" I asked after a short pause.

"Nothing wrong with my girl. She knows where to come to have
things put right. You won't find her." She hung up.

"Tell your daughter hello for me," I said into the dead phone. "Tell her I think of her often and affectionately."

I tried her again that afternoon, in person, taking off early from work. It had been two years, and we were reasonable people. I walked up to the front door wearing stockings and low-heeled pumps; I meant to meet her on her own ground. When the door swung open there was a German shepherd maintaining a steady growl, like a car in neutral, with Sally's mother a dim shape behind him.

"I just wanted to know about Sally," I said. "We're all so worried about her." It made more sense to say it this way, I reasoned. Better than *Now that I know I could see her again, I'm filled with a yearning to touch her fingertips.*

Sally's mother's voice floated from the darkness behind the dog. "If you turn around now you'll have enough time to get to your car. We know our rights. We haven't forgotten anything."

I smiled at her, held up my hands to show how peaceful I was. "We've missed her. I can't wait to see her again."

"You won't be seeing her." The dog took one calculating step.

"You don't understand," I said, backing up. "You don't need to say this." The dog took another step, his massive body quivering with restraint. His eyes were greenish, like the sky before terrible rain. "We're not enemies," I said.

"*You* don't understand," her mother said as the dog's growls darkened. "There's nothing I don't know. I will blot you out."

As I drove away I watched the windows upstairs. I might have seen a figure. Was it Sally, waving good-bye, motioning me to come back? Once her mother had borrowed a mannequin from a department store to position before windows so we thought for weeks that Sally was at home. When we'd stormed the house to find the plastic body, long fringe covering its eyes, Sally's mother had laughed and laughed. "I knew you'd be taken in," she had said. "Mothers know how to take care of their own."

I stopped at a convenience store at the bottom of the hill. It was as familiar as my own kitchen, filled with the staples of my life— quarts of milk, frozen entrees, brilliant magazines offering tips on

clothing, bed partners, never-fail cakes. HOW WOMEN ASK FOR
IT! And, next to it, TODAY'S MOTHERS: YOU CAN HAVE IT
ALL.
"But who would want it all? Just a little. Just sometimes." The
cashier looked at me warily, and I handed her two packs of gum, a
soft drink. "Dinner."
She shook her head and rattled open a sack. "Your mother would
never approve," she said.

I was late getting to Anne's apartment, and I could hear the murmur
of people before I even knocked on the door. They were ranged
around the room with newspapers, telephone books, legal pads. All
the tools from the old days. Martin had gotten fatter, and so had
Mary. Everyone looked lumpish and earthbound beside the heavy
directories and lamps, the long phone cords trailing from the walls.
Anne looked up and said, "Where are the maps?" I had of course
forgotten them.
The murmur rose, the sound of workers in accustomed concert, as
steady as an engine. There was a place for me across the coffee table
from Mary, but I was immobilized at the door, watchful and iso-
lated, the way I felt at movies when the big dance number sends
everyone on the screen swirling through the streets.
Martin was sprawled over the classifieds, his index finger tracing
every line. Once, after a month on the road with a rock and roll
band, she'd taken out an advertisement: *Bo-peep here. Sheep, do
you read me?* It took us the better part of five weeks to find her then,
asleep next to the bass player. He had his strong fingers dug into her
hair, and it fell to me to loosen the fine strands, the hardest task
of all.
"What we need is to settle on a plan," Jeff fretted, his fingers
pilling the worn upholstery. "Get her away from her mother. We
need to stake Sally out."
"Her mother has a dog," I said. "Looks mean."
"How do you know?" Anne asked, narrow-eyed.
"I went," I said. "To see her. This afternoon. Before I forgot the
maps."
The room was abruptly quiet and Anne looked at me, her face

frozen. She folded her arms and sighed chestily, tapping her fingers at her elbows. "I know," she said finally. "I realize it's been a long time. You probably thought it was a good idea to take things into your own hands." Another gusting sigh, breath enough to support a dozen small birds. "But I can't believe you don't remember we're working as a team. It will take all of our *coordinated efforts*"—she paused to glare—"to get Sally free. To save her."

This was the way, I was thinking, Sally's mother thinks about keeping her from us. She would use those very words: freedom, salvation.

"Her mother's a menace. Lunatic. She shouldn't have been allowed to have a daughter," Anne said. I had heard her say it so many times. I had said it myself.

"What would we be doing if she hadn't?" I asked. I looked at them ringed around the table, their faces lit warmly to suggest community and commitment, and I remembered Sally's mother's dog, its eyes bright with menace. The rules had changed now. Not because there was a dog, or even that we were two years gone and out of trim for the old battles. *It's not us she came to,* I wanted to say.

Andrew muttered about dinner and got up. The others bent again to their papers. I watched the telephoning begin. Most of our old numbers were no good anymore, of course, and two people hung up—one with a force I could hear across the room.

"That could mean we're getting closer," Mary said cheerily from the couch.

"That could mean her mother got there first," Jeff said, his hand to his ear.

From the kitchen floated aromas of basil and garlic, canned tomatoes. Spaghetti was the only thing Andrew could cook, his recipe and technique perfected over hundreds of nights. "More salt," Anne called out without looking up. "You never put in enough salt. Here's something: a boat show at the convention center."

"Too many people," said Jeff, dialing again.

"Lecture on extraterrestrials at UCLA," Mary said.

"Too weird. Can't you find any spiritual healers?" called Andrew from the kitchen. I could hear salt cascading. I didn't leave the door

I leaned against, didn't step into the room. Their faces were aglow, like the faces of any true believers, sure of their cues and responses. I didn't understand why they couldn't see. She was adrift away from us, and we wouldn't find her if we read every newspaper in the country.

"She could be," Anne was saying. "Or she might want to go back to the modeling place. She went back three times that one year. Whoever's got Northridge, make sure to do some surveillance. I'll take Century City to Santa Monica." She had drawn an outline of the city and was dividing it into rough kite-shaped sections. She printed a big A on the west side, then looked back at me, her face blank. "Where do you want to go?"

Crowded back, I blinked and swallowed. "I'll go everywhere. I'll be your floating member." The silence had fallen again, and the group gazed at me. "I'll drift. Keep my eyes open, see what I can see." Their faces were round and flat with surprise, and I felt the distance deepen between us, ashy and unrecoverable. So many nights. Years. And still we knew nothing of each other except the impassioned, thrilling ritual of finding Sally. I tried to remember a conversation, a shopping trip, normal human contact. There was no more connection among us than the patterns astrologists saw, those willed alliances, that imaginary unity.

"I'll be in touch," I told them, and backed out of the room, craven as a hound. But the moment the door closed I felt giddy and buoyant, as if my toes were only skinning the surface of the pavement. If anyone had breathed on me I would have sailed into the sky, my skirt belling around my knees.

It was late; the moonless sky had a dirty pinkish cast, but the spill of lights from the city was dazzling. The night had spread itself before me and I felt my freedom sharp as pain. There was nothing to keep me from dancing down boulevards, catching a plane to Havana. I could become a starlet or an aviator. I could train exotic animals, appearing in public with lavish sunglasses and a puma trailing from each wrist.

My mouth full of a taste like fire, I went straight home, without a single deviation, and once there cleansed my face, ironed a skirt for the next morning and brushed my hair fifty strokes as I had since childhood. I felt in each stroke the startled knowledge: that each moment was selection, that alone I could be whomever I chose.

That night I dreamed of Sally. She was drifting terribly away, her hair floating like a cloud around her head, and my arms ached to bring her back again. I was balancing on tall spires, hopping from one to another and calling to her, but her eyes were fixed on the sun as she levitated gracefully out of sight. I awoke panting, my hair snarled into a nest in the middle of my pillow.

At seven I left word with my secretary that I was too ill to come to the office. I showered and put on the clothes I had laid out the night before—a tidy skirt, sensible shoes. I wanted to tell Sally's mother about how it had been when we brought her daughter back from the closet-sized apartment near Chinatown. "I didn't mean to go away," she had said when we helped her to bed. "I didn't think it would be like that."

"Hush now," I'd said, working at the tangles that two weeks of neglect had put in her bright hair.

"I just wanted to find out a little." Her voice had gone sere and blank. "They said I'd like it. What would I have done if you hadn't come?"

"No need to think about that," I'd told her, and she leaned her head back and pressed her hand against my cheek. If her mother had seen that, she would have understood. We were nothing she had to protect Sally from.

The neighborhood where Sally's mother lived was full of spacious homes with expansive windows. I wasn't three feet up the walkway before the front door opened and the dog stood quivering, his front legs over the threshold and his eyes glowing. Sally's mother came out and stood behind him, her feet planted side by side on the mat.

"Hello," I said. The dog growled.

"I can call the police."

"I just happened to be driving by," I said. "Admiring your geraniums. I'd like to grow geraniums as nice as yours." I was booming the words like a whistle-stop politician. "What's your secret?"

The dog inched down the front step, his growl steady. Didn't he ever have to breathe? "My neighbor has nice flowers, and she mulches with seaweed. What do you use?" The dog edged down two more steps, the muscles around his neck defined and pulsing. "All your neighbors here must envy the things you raise. You have so many things to be envied. Real control over your life."

"This constitutes harassment." She was erect at the edge of her meticulous welcome mat, her eyes fixed beyond my head.

"No it doesn't," I said. I was stung. "It doesn't. The street's public." How could she think that? I was no harasser.

"You've been at her and at her."

"She's my friend."

Sally's mother looked at me sharply. "Then let her call you."

"You won't let her." I had spoken before I thought, and now Sally's mother was smiling nastily. The hanging plants on the porch cast a softening shadow across her forehead.

"She calls whom she pleases. She's grown. She has a husband."

"Why is she here?"

"Why are you here?"

I spoke very slowly. Pain was blossoming between my eyes, and I was trying to watch the dog. But it was all inevitable, like a nine-year-old's humiliating return home after trying to run away. This was the only place I could come. It was like a fairy tale—if I could only find the right questions, she would have to give me the answers. Not even because she wanted to, but because she was Sally's mother, and knew, and it was the order of things.

"I'm not looking for your girl."

"Don't be ridiculous," she snapped, "you'd be a fool if you weren't."

"I'm not," I said, "I'm not. I just want to talk to you." It was the truth. Her figure stood firmly in the doorway, blocking the light. She was as solid as houses.

She didn't blink, or stop watching the sky. The dog was before her like terrible statuary. "What in the world do you imagine we could talk about? I spend my life bringing my girl from harm. If you would care to please me and do right by her, you might move to Brazil. I understand there are many opportunities in the movie industry."

Brazil, I was thinking. How they would love Sally there; how easily she would go shining among them. "Have you been there?" I asked.

She snapped her head around to me. "I have a child to see to. To keep safe. You wouldn't understand that."

All the images came rushing to me—feeding warm bread to creamy-faced children, cool hands smoothing away every childhood illness, Sally's mother holding and consoling and brushing back the hair from her daughter's perfect brow. "Do you do it?" I asked. "Do you keep her safe?" Because if you do, I was thinking, I want to be the next in line.

"No one else has ever done right by her." Facing the hills to the east, she held her shoulders level as a T square. Then she turned her gaze to me, and narrowed her eyes. "I'm within my rights. You've got one minute to leave."

I looked at her for as long as I dared, memorizing her tidy dress, the neat, low heels of her squared-off shoes. There could be no chaos in a house that contained such orderly shoes. "Why is she back?" I cried out. "Why didn't she stay away?"

I was already running for the car before the dog hit his stride, and I whisked into the front seat only a step ahead of him. He bit the breeze I made slamming the door. In an upstairs window I saw a figure semaphoring; as I craned to see better, I felt the dog hurl himself against my back tire. All I could make out was a shape moving behind the glass; it weaved as if hysterical with fear or laughter. Meanwhile my car shuddered as the dog tore at the tire. He kept up with me for four blocks, snarling full tilt.

I had driven ten miles before I realized I was talking. "She's such a lovely young woman," I was saying conversationally. "We so rarely see that kind of beauty—purity, is what it is—anymore. You must be so proud.

"Of course," I said, inclining my head graciously to the empty passenger seat, "she must have been a very special child. You were able to nurture her. She certainly does have an exciting life ahead of her. And *your* life!" My laugh tinkled gaily. "I should imagine. Just to keep up with her. Well, she's a sweet thing."

With some effort, I managed to make myself stop, although dis-

jointed words broke through; "Hair!" I exclaimed. "Draperies." I
drove steadily for eight hours, stopping only twice, both times to
buy gasoline. I traveled down streets I'd never seen before, explor-
ing the tiny, broken alleys and cul-de-sacs that flourished inside
unfamiliar neighborhoods. I noticed houses, poinsettia plants grown
shoulder high.

At an intersection downtown I was caught behind a truck where
two men were unloading fashion mannequins. One of the men,
catching my eye, took the arm of his mannequin and moved it up
and down, so the figurine was waving at me. "This is not likely,"
I said aloud. "This is hardly even plausible." But he grinned and
kept waving the plastic arm until I waved back. When I pulled into
traffic again, I could see in the rearview mirror that he kept waving. For three blocks, until I was safely on the freeway again, I
fought the urge to turn around, go back and tumble them into the
back seat.

"A rage for order," I said at the turnoff to Anaheim. "The
woman has a gift for ordering." A life with boundaries and certainties in order. The fierceness of mother love, part of the natural order
of things. It was the right of every child, to know that everything, all
the universe, is in order. Even I could see that much. How could we
have imagined we were helping her? All the Errol Flynn entrances,
how we had caught her up and swept her away, but we could never
keep her. She slipped through our hands like wind. I saw it all now,
now I had a grip on it—how wrong we had been for so long. The
good manager, I had learned in the office, *anticipates* problems, the
unreliable stars, the broken contracts. "It was an understandable
mistake," I said to the car. She used to call us and weep beautifully.
It would take a mother to hold out against such tears. I nearly turned
the car then and there to find her, to tell Sally's mother I understood
now. Instead, I sped home, my weary body feeling small and infi-
nitely vulnerable in the flow of the crowded city.

There was a message from Anne on the machine. "We've found her.
Come if you're coming." I stood at the table for a long time, my
finger holding down the stop button.

We'd found her once in a tenement hallway, a boy who'd told her to call him Jesus collapsed across her lap. When she saw us she said, "I would have been all alone if you hadn't come. I need you so." When I took her hand I could feel the pulse charging in the hollow of her wrist. I had trailed her erratic passage for so long—crossed and recrossed territory in spindling, complex patterns, headlong as a roller coaster.

By the time I telephoned Anne it was two-thirty in the morning, and when I told her I would try to meet them she snapped, "Don't do us any favors." I heard the sound of her slammed receiver for several minutes after the connection was broken.

The next morning, when I called again in contrition, she told me to go to the Holiday Inn in Pasadena. "There's a troupe of Hawaiian dancers there who swallow fire while they hula. They're going back to the islands soon—we have to hurry."

"Has anyone seen her there?"

"Where else could she be?" Anne asked.

But I couldn't find it again, the old faith. The lines and girders had snapped. *She calls whom she pleases,* her mother had said. I thought of the great broad expanse of the city, its thousands of private drives nurturing Lana Turners and other unimaginable secrets. People all over Los Angeles County danced in their living rooms to Xavier Cugat records. It wasn't as if the only fire-eaters would be in Pasadena.

All day, I fielded calls. An agent named Marty whined, "This girl, you can't believe her. You have to see her to believe her." He had been calling me for a week, despite my steady insistence that I had nothing to do with casting. "You see her, you'll find a way to have something to do with casting," he said. "Let me tell you, you'll see this girl. She's a comer. And you'll be sick that you let her get away. Sick."

"You would be amazed," I told him, "at what I've let go."

Still, I went to the Holiday Inn that night, even knowing that Sally wouldn't be there, knowing that all the wanting in the world wouldn't produce her for me. Knowing myself to be already unmoored, like a kite snapped free of its cord. For the first time since

I'd carried her up my apartment house stairs, I was truly alone, without pattern or habit, and I felt weightless, vulnerable to every shifting current and cold, cold wind.

Inside, the others were sprinkled around the lounge. Martin sported a penciled-in moustache that made him look languid and feline. I seated myself next to Anne at the bar. "What do we do if she's here with her mother?"

"Divide and conquer." Anne's eyes gleamed. Her eyes were raking through the dark, looking for Sally's white skin, skin that held the impression of a bruise for weeks. So soft under the hand, no one could ever forget. And eyes like glass. I imagined her mother looking through a window. Her iron face.

"You know what?" I said, too softly for Anne to hear me. "She's not going to be here tonight."

I wandered back outside, leaving Anne counting tables and muttering strategies. I missed Sally now with desperation; my hands were sparked with the need to feel the slight weight of that yielding body. What role could I have in the world, without her soft presence?

I walked for blocks. It was a loud, overlit strip, without a trace of the old land that had been broad and gracious. The street was meant for cars now, and I passed four parking lots in a block. The air was murky, tea-colored, and smelled of exhaust and hot grease. At the Holiday Inn, I calculated, the show would be beginning. I drifted down the sidewalk, peering into shop windows, trying to imagine the people—so many! It would take an army—who changed the displays, wrenched the mannequins into new positions. I didn't know how far I'd gone or where I was when I came to a small grocery store, but I pushed in the front door as if I came every week, and had the right.

There was the smell of bread loosely sealed, and oranges. The store was bright and old-fashioned, with packages of breakfast cereal and detergent, and I thought I would buy something as a reward, a respite from the dirt and noise beyond the door. And so I dawdled down aisles, inspecting hair cream and eggs, sniffing at the bars of soap and boxes of crayons for their clean, waxy scents. I picked up aerosol cans and put them back—they would be unpleasant to carry in the night, such slick canisters. What I wanted was something to hold in my palms: walnuts or new potatoes, rough or grooved surfaces to roll against my skin. I raised my eyes toward the deep produce bins, and I saw Sally at the end of the store, sitting on the edge of the barrel that held apples, swinging her legs. Of course, I thought. How could it have taken me so long? Things had changed; the old days of weeping phone calls had passed. The only way to find Sally was not to look for her.

There was a hand around my arm, and Sally's mother's voice. "Get out," she said. But Sally was smiling at me, her pale hands buried in apples. "You have nothing to do here. Do you think I would just let you carry off my daughter?"

I had so much to say to Sally's mother. I had to find all the words to tell her that I understood now, I was through fighting. I was here to *join* her. I knew all this, and instead of saying any of it, I smiled at Sally. Her eyes were fixed in my direction, and I was so happy I could scarcely breathe. With my free arm, I waved to her, slow and stiff as the sign at a railroad crossing.

"You don't have a chance," Sally's mother said. "She already left a husband. She won't come now to you."

"Why did she come home?" I didn't stop smiling at Sally, couldn't turn from her, even though she didn't run to me, even though she didn't wave or cry out or perhaps even see me. Why should she? It wasn't her part. She existed to be seen. It was her mother who recognized me, who reached out. I could feel the pressure of her mother's fingers on my arm as I waved. "She came for you, didn't she?" I said. "She wouldn't come for me."

"She came where she was safe. I won't let anyone touch her. Alone out there—he struck her. He struck my girl." I watched Sally's hands brush over the tops of apples, and how they shone. "Took her in marriage to love and protect, and slapped her ear till the blood came."

"Well, of course." Everything seemed very clear. In the bright and nutritious air I felt enlightened. I watched Sally, her body like water, her eyes like air. No one could see her and not yearn. And he had had vows on his side: to have, hold. "Anything perfect will suffer," I said.

Sally's mother stiffened. "What are you trying to make of us?" she hissed. "What are you trying to do?" She spun away from me, back to her post next to the tomatoes, close enough to touch her daughter's shadow, and so I had no chance to tell her that I wasn't trying to make anything, that she and her daughter were made when I came to them. A mother with her feet on the ground, a daughter with eyes like the sky. I watched Sally's mother reach out to straighten her daughter's sleeve, her thumb pressing for a moment against Sally's arm. The spot was red when she moved her hand away, even from such slight pressure. A lifetime of marks, of damage, I was thinking, from even a mother's hands on skin so delicate. The red spots bloomed. Amazing that he had held back so long.

I waited, leaning back against the ledge that held dense, lunar cauliflowers. A woman came down the aisle with a rattling grocery cart. Looking at Sally, she started, then smiled. Sally held out an apple and the woman said, "Oh, thank you," and stood looking up at that face that was pale as the sky.

Sally bent to her as if to whisper a secret. "It's a promotion," she said, her hair falling in a clean sheet beside her face. "For apples. Take some for your family. Take some for yourself."

She still swung her legs, beating out a light rhythm against the barrel, and she handed the woman two more. From the far end of the aisle, past sweet rolls sticky against their cellophane, there came another woman, heavy on her feet, her mouth straining and ugly as a fish. Sally's hand selected an apple. It was gorgeous in her hand.

"Special," she murmured to the woman. "Only fifty-nine cents a pound."

The woman smiled at her, dimly.

"You could make a pie," said Sally, and the woman nodded. "You could make two pies."

Her mother didn't turn around, but I would not let her close me out. I had new understanding, I had the strength of my young body. She shifted her weight, her back stern before me, and I shifted mine. When she raised her hand as if to correct or signal her daughter, I raised mine too, and when she crossed the aisle to rearrange Sally's skirt, I silently went to straighten the opposite edge. Underneath, I saw Sally's slender legs, her feet tender and delicate. Her mother and I backed away while Sally held apples before her like riches.

I would show her. I would learn; I was a quick study, from good stock. I would learn to walk with swift and sure steps, firm on the earth.

Together, we could keep her. We would keep her held and safe. No one, not even a mother, lived forever—had Sally's mother thought of that? Someone would need to carry on. I was ready now, ready to learn about things that were solid and deep, that stayed in place, that lasted.

Sally's hands dug into the bin. She held up apples, breathed on them, murmured to them. When a Rome Beauty fell from her long fingers, her mother and I dashed together to retrieve it. Her mother wouldn't allow me to touch it, but I cupped my palm underneath the other woman's. Half-kneeling before the apples, we raised our faces and waited for Sally's smile.

Bodies at Sea

After Andrea had heard and overheard the consolations so many times that she awakened nights hearing, "So young! So young!" sounding in the sodden air over the bed, she understood that she had to leave. She nursed no particular bitterness. It was simply true: There was no place amidst the bright streets and grocery stores for a twenty-five-year-old widow.

She was not, she insisted always, single again. The subject came up at dinners, shopping expeditions—even at the reception after the funeral. "After all, you're so young," her mother's friend had said. "Times are different now. He wouldn't have wanted you to bury yourself." Andrea stared, thinking that she had surely misheard.

"Plenty of time," her aunt said later, "to start a new life." She smiled conspiratorially, and Andrea excused herself, went to wash her face. What were people trying to do to her?

She ignored the advice she received in the weeks after Kevin died, at twenty-eight, of cancer—there was no reason to remove her rings or cut her hair. She wore the dresses he had liked and remembered his smile when she put them on. She kept her job, took on more hours. She managed a kind of life for eight months, pulling herself hand over hand through each day, and then she found she could pull no further. Her mother's neighbor, explaining that she had loved Andrea since she was a child, offered to introduce her to a young man, her nephew, an engineer. "You're so young," she'd said, beginning to weep a little. "I can't bear to see you do this to yourself."

Do? All she was doing was living each day.

"It's not as if you'd been married for years and years."

"No," Andrea said. "We were hardly married at all."

"You can't just stop here."

"No." *Stop,* she thought. It had been a difficult day at the store, a day of horrid children. One entire display had toppled. *Stop right here.* After she finally returned home and went to bed, she awakened screaming, and in the morning she gave the floor manager her notice.

"I'm so glad," her mother said on the phone. "I really think this is the right decision. You need a new start, away from all the memories."

"The road to recovery," Andrea said.

"That's right."

"No more of this unhealthy morbidity. After a few months, I should be able to forget I was ever married."

"No one's asking you to forget Kevin. But you've been—mourning. It's not your life that's ended. You've got to get on with things."

Andrea set her jaw.

"Kevin would be happy to know that you're moving on. He wouldn't have wanted you mooning around a year after."

Oh yes he would, she wanted to say. He would have wanted her to stay put, right there, remembering. She would have expected as much from him. They had lived together three years, they had had weight and substance. They had had *plans!* She closed her eyes, clenched hard the hand on the counter. "Eight months," she said.

"Well," her mother said. Then, "Where will you go?"

Startled, forgetting herself, Andrea almost told her. She coughed delicately and said, "West."

"West?"

"I've always wanted to live near the ocean."

"That's right, you have," her mother said. Her voice was full of doubt. Andrea had never told her mother any such thing. "But so far."

"That's the best thing for me. A fresh start. Blank slate, new broom. None of these damaging memories."

"Well," her mother said. "You can always call. Make sure you call."

Andrea packed one suitcase that night, putting into it clothes she rarely wore and one shirt of Kevin's; the rest of it—clothes, blenders, furniture, books—she left. She stayed up late, washing towels and sheets, and when she finally lay down she slept on the bare mattress, clean bedding folded and piled on the dresser across the room. She dreamed that night of Kevin, as she had every night since his death.

Before Andrea married Kevin she spent evenings with Martin Chelney. They had met when she was still in high school, he already in college, sorting mail and stock at the shipping company where she typed on Saturday mornings. At first, he took her out for ice cream, then later, after she graduated, for coffee. Always they came back to his apartment, where they would sit at his kitchen table and talk.

"Where do you see yourself in five years?" he would ask her. She couldn't imagine. At seventeen, five years had been an enormity, beyond the grasp of mortals. Married, she supposed. A house. Linens, china.

"Peru!" he would say. "Nepal! Photographing emus. If people could just *see*—we can do whatever we want." Andrea was dazzled. No one had ever talked to her like this, and when she came home at night she was giddy with it, silly as if she'd been drinking. Telling her about the untapped potential of the antarctic, of Jupiter's moons, his big arms swam through the air. His fingers traced maps for her over the surface of the table. "Can you see it? Can you see how it could be?" Hydraulics, lasers, solar and wind power. She could. She could see it.

He would stop then, look up suddenly. "What are *you* thinking? What do you think all day?" At first she'd been shy, imagining she should tell him *Thermodynamics. I've been thinking about thermodynamics since I got up,* but she learned that he meant it. He listened carefully as she told him about her teachers, her supervisor, her mother, her friends. He consoled her, took her side. He gave advice.

He remembered names, asked about tests. He seemed as content talking about her argument in the lunchroom as he did talking about rural industrialization, and Andrea came to save things for him, the details of her days, until nothing seemed real before she'd shared it with him.

Even after Martin married Paula he and Andrea talked night after night—when at first Andrea had held back, Martin called her, hurt. "Where have you been? I haven't heard from you all week."

"I thought you might want to be with your wife."

"She'll be here. Do you need me to pick you up?" And she had gone, and sat at the table with Martin to discuss astral projection and nuclear-free zones. He had shaken the hair from his eyes impatiently, slapped his flat palms on the table and his legs. All it took was vision. They could change the way people lived, they could change the world. Paula slipped quietly in and out, a vague smile on her face. Andrea scarcely noticed her. She had only the filmiest sense of their daily life, whether Martin ate breakfast, how he and Paula shared the car, but she knew Martin's dreams, the ideas that entranced and captured him. They had gone on without change for so long, she assumed they would go on talking forever. It wasn't until the packing boxes were actually in the apartment that he told her about moving to California.

"It's the right thing," he said evasively, tracing the wood grain over the table. "Things will be better there." He was subdued and didn't meet her eyes, and for the first time in the months since he'd been married Andrea was aware of Paula welling up between them like fog.

"I'll write to you," Martin said the night before he left, as they stood in the jumble of furniture and heaped clothing. He looked steadily at Andrea while Paula stacked boxes she had carried in from other rooms. "I'll write about it all."

He wrote her a week later, and then two months after that. The letters came at irregular intervals, but they were always long, full of descriptions and conversations Martin had had with people at work, in stores, along the beach. In the spring after he left, when Andrea married Kevin, he wrote eight pages about Pacific tidal patterns. Months would go by without any word, and then he would send four letters in two weeks. Andrea would hold the letters, read them again and again. She would try to find the encoded messages that explained why he was suddenly driven to write page after page.

There had been no letters since Kevin died. Andrea hadn't realized that she was waiting, but since the night she awakened screaming it had been clear that she had to talk to Martin. She wouldn't know what to do until she'd heard his low voice, watched his hands clumsily wing through the air.

She hadn't called, knowing that once she was there the words would come. She would tell Martin about people, her friends and relatives; he was the one who could take up for her, set things right. She wanted to tell him about the evenings, when she set in motion every appliance she owned to drive out the apartment's stillness. Everything became clearer as she drove, the clouds dissolving overhead. She wanted to tell him things. Her letters to Martin had been small and plain—she had written when she took the job at the clothing store, when Kevin was considered for promotion. Now it was time to say everything else, to explain, and Andrea drove faster and faster toward the ocean.

It was Paula who opened the door. In four years she had changed beyond recognition—had Andrea not seen Martin's reassuring bulk behind her, she would have murmured apologies and fled. The woman had narrowed, everything about her gone slit-shaped and mean. She sat on a stool in a corner of the kitchen while Martin fetched glasses and Andrea leaned against the refrigerator, waiting. After the long drive she was primed, the pent-up words ready to spill forth. Four years! A marriage. There was so much to say.

Paula began to talk before Andrea could say anything. "I have lost three babies in two years," she announced.

"I'm sorry," Andrea said, taking a step back. The words were automatic. She was good at condolence now, a past master—she nearly added, *So young, so young.* Martin kept his back turned as he worked ice cubes from their trays.

"I know what you're thinking," Paula said, leering forward from the stool so that Andrea stepped back again. "You're thinking what we'd do with a baby."

"Do?" Andrea asked. She glanced at Martin, waiting for him to answer. What could she, newly bereaved, be expected to say to this woman who craned hungrily forward on her stool?

"People always wonder what we would do with a baby. They look at us and say, 'Why, what would you do with a baby?' They say it every time."

"People," Andrea said, "say the most incredible things."

"They say, 'What would you do with a baby?' " Paula repeated, staring at her.

"Isn't that terrible."

"No," Paula said, her mouth working into a long smirk, "you don't get it. They really don't know. Maybe we'd hang him out like a flag." She snickered. "Maybe we'd use him to hold up books."

Andrea looked at Martin again. He was filling glasses with ice and soda water.

"Three times," Paula said.

Martin turned with the glasses in his hands. "Andrea is here because her husband died. Let's see if she doesn't have anything else she wants to talk about," he said.

They stood shoulder to shoulder and looked at her. Andrea shrugged, awkward as a teenager. Movies? Good books? The other woman watching her with a glaring, discordant grin, she could hardly start in telling everything about Kevin, the sharp pain that never stopped, never; she lifted her soda water.

"Mud in your eye," said Paula and drained her glass.

Martin had given Andrea no warnings or hints before he married Paula—he had given her nothing at all. He told her with a gentleness that had been insulting of his plans to marry, and after that never mentioned her again. When Andrea came to see him he would greet her at the door as he always had, and she only glimpsed Paula behind him, arms filled with snowy linen, busy with a thousand household tasks.

Andrea had tried at first to watch her and understand what it was about this soft-looking woman that had pulled Martin to her side, but she was always hastening in and out of rooms, leaving behind her the smells of starched cloth and yeast, and Martin was always talking, reaching out, sometimes, to take Andrea's hand—she could only focus on one thing at a time. In the end, she nearly forgot about Paula, dismissed her like the mothers of friends at whose houses she'd spent afternoons in high school.

That night, when Martin and Paula showed Andrea to the spare room, there were linens piled on the end of the bed, a glass and a pitcher on the bedside table.

"Are you a nighttime drinker?" Paula said. "If you are, get your water now. It's California water, you know, so it'll make you crazy." Andrea, reasonably sure she was joking, smiled, but Paula kept staring at her implacably. Martin, standing behind her, said nothing.

"No," Andrea said. "I never wake up thirsty."

"Okay," said Paula, turning around and leaving the room.

"Sleep tight," said Martin.

Andrea listened after she got into bed, but she could hear nothing from them. She didn't know how to interpret the silence—was it fury with her sudden arrival? Perhaps they had merely retreated to opposite ends of the house, engaged in tasks that excluded each other. Perhaps they too had gone to bed, and were making love silently, out of respect for her. Perhaps they were always silent with each other, even after so long, time enough to learn to talk.

Andrea, lying still, longed for any noise—a drawer pulled, a lamp switched on or off. In the dense quiet, the intimacy of their shared life rose before her like a wall. How could she have imagined it wouldn't matter? Rapidly, as if projected on a screen, she remembered Kevin's face as they had walked together, sung, slept—in a hundred attitudes of love. The dearness of him, sharp as glass, as he had read a newspaper, frowning through the hair in his eyes. She could talk to Martin for a week, she thought, and never explain or translate. What words were there for the perfect intricacy of lives locked together like clocks?

She and Kevin had never had silence. They had rushed to each other at night, impatient to share the sights they had seen that day, the facts they'd learned. They had laughed, sung with the radio, danced clumsily across the linoleum. When they made love they shouted, pounded on furniture and the floor. Remembering Kevin's touch, Andrea felt the loss again as if new, and her body curled in the small bed. Nevertheless, she strained to hear in the clear silence. She yearned. She was fretful as a child with the desire to belong, to understand everything, to know all the things Martin and Paula knew. When she finally fell asleep, the only sound she could hear was the unfamiliar pull and wash of heavy waves on the sand.

In the morning Andrea waited until she heard the clatter of cups from the kitchen before she left her room. She felt wretched, her body and head aching from the long drive and uneasy night, and she hoped that it was Martin she heard running water. *It'll make you crazy.* She believed it. Paula had reared up in her dreams, laughing and plucking thin children from her side. There had been no sign of Martin or Kevin, just Paula's wounded body yielding babies like fruit.

It was Paula in the kitchen, wearing a bikini. She glanced up at Andrea, then went back to washing dishes.

"Good morning," said Andrea. There was no response other than the squeak of the washcloth over plates. Andrea looked for a coffeepot, but the counters were clean and bare. "Is there any coffee?" she asked.

"Have you ever lost a child?" Paula asked conversationally.

Andrea sank into a chair, a hand at her thumping temple. "No." Paula was silent, her eyes small. "My husband and I were, well, waiting. To have a family. We didn't know about the cancer until just before the end." This had been another source of endless consolation. *How sorry you must be,* people had said, one after the other. *How sad that you don't at least have his child to carry on.*

"I thought maybe you had. It makes a bond, you know." She turned her attention back to the dishes and began to whistle the theme from *Oklahoma!*

Andrea said, "Excuse me—do you have any coffee?"

Paula, still whistling, shook her head.

"Is Martin up?" Paula's whistling shrilled when she came to the cowboys' whoops. Either she hadn't heard or she was ignoring the question; she went through two choruses and rinsed the sink before she turned around again.

"What do you want to know about it?"

"What?"

"Losing three children. What do you want to know?"

Andrea felt as if murky waters were spinning up under her chin.
"Is Martin here?" she asked, sounding even to herself as timid as
a little girl.

Paula grinned slyly. "Martin? I don't know where Martin is."
Keeping her eyes on Andrea she reached around for the dishwashing
liquid, squeezed a small amount on her fingertips and began to
massage the thick fluid onto her stomach. "Liquid like this breaks
down the salt in the air," she said. "It protects the skin. Everyone
in California has a terrific body, have you noticed that?"

"You don't know where he is? When do you think he'll come
in?"

"People don't have children. They go to the beach to run. They
bring their dogs with them."

"Martin. Where is he?" Her voice was thickening, crowded with
panic. Alone in the kitchen with this sly-eyed woman smeared with
heavy liquid—there would be knives, in a kitchen.

"They call the other ones B.A.S."

"Please," said Andrea.

"B.A.S. Bodies At Sea. For people who can't control their
bodies." She whistled a single piercing note. "Get it?"

"Stop," said Andrea.

"You don't want to know anything. Why don't you want to know
anything?" She grinned and began to advance on Andrea, her
gummy fingers describing tiny circles before her, and Andrea edged
out of her chair, stepped back, nearer the door.

"Just tell me about Martin. I'll leave, come back later." And
then, as Paula came a step closer, "I don't want it. Whatever it is
you know. I know things too. I hate knowing." When she bolted
from the room she ran with all of her force so that she couldn't stop
herself at the front door and slammed into Martin, who said nothing
as Andrea wept and clung to him and Paula whistled again, high and
shrill.

Andrea tried to make him go away with her then, on the spot,
begging and crying while he gently loosened her frantic grasp. "I

must—I can't—You—'' She had no idea what she was trying to say. Paula, reeking of soap, danced around them, her whistle giving way before long to high laughter.

"I'll always be your friend," Martin said to Andrea, who cried, "Friends *talk!* You have to talk to me!"

"We do talk," he said. "We'll talk some more."

"What will you talk about?" asked Paula. She pointed at Andrea. "You don't want to know things." Turning to Martin she said conspiratorially, "She hates knowing."

Martin stood behind his wife, who glistened with gluey soap. Her body was so reduced that Andrea was reminded of the hysterical throats of young birds.

"Now, me—I love knowing. I know things now I never would have dreamed. I know things about children and I know things about Martin. I even know things about widows. It's all very interesting."

Paula was rubbing more dishwashing liquid over her shoulders. Andrea closed her eyes. She could feel their eyes on her, standing alone as Paula massaged the blue liquid into her skin.

"My mother taught me how to make the lightest biscuits in the world," Paula said. "I was going to teach my children so they would always be able to make biscuits. But I don't have children, I lose them. Nobody to teach biscuits to."

When Andrea looked up, Paula's teeth glittered. "Why did you come here?" Paula asked.

Martin was looking away, over both their heads toward the ocean. Andrea turned to him. "I just lost my husband. I wanted to talk to you."

"But I'm the one who knows," Paula said. "Not Martin. He's not the one who loses things."

Martin's gaze was fixed, like a blind man's. Andrea felt as if she should cry out to him, call and call until from his far distance he would hear her and shout in return. "Why did you come here?" she asked him sadly. "Why did you leave?"

"He thought it would be good for us to find new direction," Paula said, her smile wide as a blade. "He told me he wanted to make a new life. So we did it. Don't you wish you could make a new life too?'' She ducked from under Martin's hands and danced back to the kitchen, working her shoulders as she began to whistle again. Andrea watched Martin look at the misty horizon. His body hung slack, as if suspended by a wire, and there was no sign of the heated vision that had once kept them, night after night, pressing each other's hands and talking about what they imagined life must bring.

She wanted to tumble his bulky body into her lap and cradle him, she wanted to whisper hushed, reassuring words. She yearned to reach and hold him, and her arms rose—if he would just look at her she would gather him in. They stood, her empty arms reaching, his dull gaze intent on the distant blue. Then he sighed, patted her arm, and followed his wife's shrill whistle into the kitchen.

Because it had a door she could close, Andrea retreated to the extra bedroom. Seated on the bed she could see sky and palm fronds from the small window. She could see seagulls, their beaks half open and their screams bright and raucous.

Occasionally she could hear light steps hurrying past her door, and once she heard the front door close. That was all. Paula and Martin, if they communicated, did so by telepathy or sign language. No one looked in to offer food or sympathy. She slipped out to the bathroom once and filled her pitcher with water from the tap, and she sipped as she watched the birds in the pale sky.

She had meant to leave as soon as she heard Paula go out. She would go anywhere, leave behind these damaged people. But she remained even after she heard the door—it might have been Martin going, leaving her unprotected against his wife, she couldn't be sure. For the moment she was content to sit undisturbed with tepid water and a view of the sky. It was peaceful, the light slanting bright and clear across the carpet. The room was still, the light buoyant, and Andrea sat so quietly she could hear her own steady pulse. She considered becoming an anchorite, cross-legged in a southern California townhouse, drinking only tap water and speaking no longer to anyone. That would be the source of her wisdom; she would explain to the world if she only could speak.

It was Martin, she reflected now, who was to blame. Paula, the lost children—had she known, she never would have come. She understood about loss. But how could she have been expected to know, even to imagine? He had written about whales, beachcombers, the flood of jellyfish that had washed onto the shore once, badly stinging dozens of bathers—but never a word about his wife, how her eyes were brilliant with unnatural light.

She stayed on the bed until the sky was quite dark. There was still no sound from Paula or Martin—no voices, not even a rustle. Maybe she had been alone all day. They might have left her the keys to the car, the deed to the house. Andrea had become hungry, and thirsty—the water was long gone—so she uncrossed her stiff legs and went out to the kitchen, where at the table Martin was waiting for her. It was the first time since she came that she'd seen him without Paula. The shock of it was almost enough to make her run back to the room.

"Been sleeping?" he said.

"No. Watching seagulls."

He nodded. "I do that." There was a pause then. Martin looked at his hands.

"Where's Paula?" she said.

He shook his head. "I don't know." Then, "You want a cup of coffee? I could make some coffee."

"That would be nice."

She watched him make his way around the kitchen, pulling the coffee maker from a cupboard, measuring water and grounds. "Old times, to drink coffee together," he said.

"Just like."

They were silent then until he brought the coffee to the table in mugs. After he sat down he said softly, "I'm sorry about Kevin."

Andrea's hand, cradled around the hot cup, jerked. Couldn't he see it was no place for such talk, the air still quivering from the morning's violence? It was wrong even to hear Kevin's name in the room. "Yes," she said.

"I know it must be, well, devastating. I can't imagine what it must be like."

Andrea looked at him. His head hung heavily between his shoulders, and his eyes were small with lack of sleep. "Can't you?" she said. "Seems to me you've learned a thing or two about loss." She heard herself—it was coming out wrong, as if to hurt him. "Martin," she said more gently, "you should have told me. I wish you'd told me."

He stared at his mug without touching it. "I didn't know what to say. It was easier not to say it. It was *better* not to say it. You know? It was better to think about other things." His voice was slow and he wouldn't look at her.

"I told you things," she said. "I told you things that happened, even if they weren't important."

He shook his head. "I told you things too. I didn't tell you anything that wasn't important."

"Paula is going crazy," she said flatly. "You didn't tell me that. Three miscarriages! How could you not have told me?"

"Two," he said. "Two miscarriages. I only knew about one until you got here. She had the other baby."

Andrea looked down, remembering months without letters, and the gentle peace of the bedroom. Her tongue was suddenly sticky in her mouth. "Crib death?" she asked softly.

When Martin didn't respond she felt the warm, liquid rush of pity. The losses are so hard, she thought. How can we hope to stand under them? She reached her hand toward his face, and he said, "When Paula came out of the delivery room a nurse said he was the most beautiful baby she'd ever seen. She said she'd never seen a newborn with such big eyes, so bright. She said, 'He looks like he's happy about being here.'"

He paused, and when he spoke again, his words were careful and measured as beads. "Paula told her to take him. She said, 'We don't know what to do with a baby.' She held him up until he cried and the nurse took him, and Paula refused to look at him again." Martin was studying his hands very carefully. With his shoulders hunched around his ears, he looked like a bear. Tamed, and dimly confused. Andrea shut her eyes. She was dizzy, and felt as if she'd been assaulted, violated in spaces she hadn't even known she contained. "Dear God. Your *child.*" She had to stop, collect herself, imagining Martin's own boy, imagining that sweet weight. "But surely she didn't take him. She couldn't have."

Martin stared at the table. "I couldn't make Paula take him home," he said, his voice guttural, like something rotted through. "She kept saying we didn't have any business keeping anybody. That's what she said while she was in labor. When she asked me what we'd do with a baby, I didn't know what to tell her. That's what I told people when they asked. Paula wouldn't talk to anyone, so that's what I told them all."

She looked at Martin's face, punched in with anguish, and she was suddenly furious. It wasn't he who was crazy, not he dancing before her and laughing. *You know better,* she wanted to shout at him. *You know. You feed a baby and bathe him. You make his way in the world.* There was no mystery here. *"You* could have taken him. You could have taken him away." Martin's son—his son!—was alive, being raised by someone who even yet couldn't imagine how she had come by him, this beautiful boy. Andrea clenched her hands to steady herself and Martin raised his bloodshot eyes to her.

"I can't raise a baby by myself."

"Why not?" she snapped, frantic with the thought of it.

"I couldn't go off by myself. I wouldn't know what to do, alone."

"You'd raise up your son," Andrea said, rushing, the words crashing like water. "You'd claim him. He's your own boy."

"And Paula's," said Martin very softly. "He's Paula's own boy."

It took nothing to see it, Paula's sticky, vibrating body, the very bones cutting into any baby she held. Her whistle, harsh and high, over an infant's wail. "You know you've got to leave her," she said, and Martin said nothing.

"Martin, you can see it, don't tell me you can't. She'll make you crazy. She might kill you, who knows? She gave away your baby."

"She's my wife."

"She gave away your *son.*"

Martin began to draw with his finger on the table. He drew long, intersecting lines, working against the grain of the wood. He said, with enormous diffidence, "Should I go with you?"

It was what she had waited, come here for. It was what she had always thought. For a moment, she had the sensation she was bobbing, a cork over deep water. "No," Andrea said.

He nodded, kept drawing, and after a long pause said, "That's what I thought." Line after line was traced, a pattern of great complexity. "When I'm alone," he said, "I think of the baby. He's fourteen months old. I read books, to see what fourteen-month-old babies do. His motor coordination is good now. He's beginning to say words, maybe even put together phrases. He's beginning to look at patterns—shapes and colors."

He glanced up at Andrea. "When I'm with Paula, I don't think about him. She—" he batted his hand vaguely through the air, "—distracts. It isn't what you say. It isn't so bad." Line after line over the top of the table. "We have a life together, we made it. That's how it's supposed to be."

Wildly, Andrea thought of Kevin. Would he have been sitting at tables, tracing invisible patterns, would she have given away their babies? She was clenching her hands bloodless. She had to clear her throat twice to find voice enough to ask what he was drawing.

"Paula. I'm writing her name. It's a habit I got into—makes me feel like I'm bringing her home."

"Does it work?"

"She comes home."

Andrea was ready to say *She won't always,* but she stopped herself. She didn't know that. Maybe Paula would come home this very minute, her arms filled with grocery sacks, exclaiming at the price of broccoli. Anything might happen. Andrea turned to the door, leaving Martin alone and tracing back his wife.

Outside the air was cool and sharp with salt. A breeze whipped Andrea's hair into her mouth. She walked quickly, turning down streets until she came to the broad boulevard that ran along the ocean. The waves shone as they broke over the sand, and the water further out glittered with the reflected lights of barges. Andrea could feel salt accumulating on her skin as she crossed the wide street, the wind stinging her eyes, and she made her way down the steep bank to the water.

The sand was smooth and cool. She walked at the edge where it crumbled with moisture, so the waves washed just inches away from her feet. Standing so close, she could see that the waves gave off their own greenish light—the phosphorescence, Martin had written once, came from dead plankton. There was light enough to see the shapes of debris—ropes of seaweed, wood fragments, a plastic cup. Martin had a son, and Paula had given him away. She shouldn't have had to know this.

Andrea crumbled the sand with her toes and looked out over the ocean. If she were out far from land, she thought, she would be able to see the reflections of stars, points of light bobbing on the dark water, and it would be beautiful. She could see the appeal for the boys who ran away to ships, even those swimmers who crossed from France to England at night, when the boats were docked. She herself was tempted to wade in until her skirt was lifted to her shoulders. She was a poor swimmer, but she could surely float in this water that was shot with light. Instead, she burrowed her toes further into the damp sand; the water, she knew, was chill.

The wind was colder and sharper at the water's edge. If Kevin were with her, Andrea thought, he would be pulling her back up the beach, toward noise and warmth. He had always hated the cold; she had seen him weep from earaches. He would bribe her indoors with promises of hot drinks, bed. Andrea stood at the edge of the ocean, her feet half buried in cold sand and her throat dense with salt, looking out over the glittering water. She stayed even after the tide had turned and the water slipped away from her.

A Thief

No one, looking at her, would have guessed Evelyn to be a woman with pets. She was not generous or immediate with her affections, not quick to call after the dogs and cats she saw as she walked to campus. She did not gravitate toward other people's animals in the way that women with babies are helpless to resist tender, new skin and fists like blossoms.

Evelyn was a clean woman, sternly tidy. Her house and the cottage behind it sat perfectly square and trim, washed every year, painted every other. Her sweaters smelled of naphtha, and the crease in her trousers hung sharp and specific. She often ran stiff fingers through the dogs' hair and rested her chin on the plush bellies of the cats, but when she stood again she was immaculately, crisply groomed. The animals, for their part, were devoted to her, capering and ecstatic every afternoon when she came home, sniffing her pockets in the vain hope of tidbits. They understood their roles, she might have said if asked.

She did not speak down to them. Evelyn knew only one language, and she relied on it to carry her through all of her life, classroom lectures and conversations with her colleagues and instructions to the employees at the dry-cleaning service. For the brief time that she had been an aunt, she had spoken thus to her tiny nephew, with his pink, plump skin and his wandering eyes the color of old-fashioned laundry bluing. "Hello," she had said to him as she said now to her quivering, ebullient pets. "It was a tedious day. I'm relieved to be home at last."

The animals, accustomed to her unflagging diction and meticulous pronunciation, romped in tight circles as Evelyn made her way to the bedroom, adjusting the folds of her coat so it hung properly in the closet, folding the blouse she had worn that day before placing it in the laundry basket. She talked to them. "Teaching is always the most difficult in the spring. I resent lecturing in classes from which half the students are missing. The students who do attend gaze out the window. Do they imagine they are unique? We would all prefer to be outside."

The slimmer of the cats, a male, balanced at the edge of the windowsill, twitching his tail invitingly. After a moment of feigned indifference during which the female examined the tufted hair between the pads of her feet, she leaped after him, missing his tail by the merest breath. The two cats fell heavily to the carpet and careened under the bed, the black dog inches behind them, jamming himself under the bedframe up to his ribcage. "It is difficult to ignore this," Evelyn said. "Their final examination grades will suffer, of course."

She donned cotton trousers and a light blouse, the clothes she used for walking the dogs. She pulled on the walking shoes she had bought in England two years before, the leather clean and brushed, still supple from saddle soap lathered over them monthly. The dogs scampered heavily around her, recognizing her walking costume, as she tied a scarf over her head. Before she left the bedroom to get their leashes Evelyn paused to slip on the bracelet that she had taken from the pocket of a student's jacket that afternoon.

Evelyn had not taken the bracelet at the prompting of a whim, some fancy that accompanied the dizzying late March air and the fragrant petals showering from ornamental plum trees all across the city. Evelyn had been systematically rifling the pockets of her students' jackets for months. Until now she had not found anything that pleased her. The usual cache was stubbed pencils, ballpoint pens whose tops were chewed into grotesque distortion, crumpled notes or cigarette packs, and, occasionally, revolting bits of food. She had learned to be careful about investigating strange pockets since the morning she had thrust her hand into an open lump of something with the consistency of cold gravy and the smell of old fish. But this time she had touched smooth, cool metal, closed her hand around it and slipped it easily into her handbag, as if she knew what to do, as if she'd been taking things of value all her life.

It was remarkably simple; it was scarcely even thrilling. Students left their belongings draped over the armchairs and sofas in the wide central lounge while they went to get lunch or newspapers. Those who remained were intent on each other, or on their notes and books; they never so much as glanced up when Evelyn passed, even when she walked before a window brilliant with morning sun and her severe shadow cut across the length of a sofa. She would stoop to pick up a jacket whose sleeve sagged onto the floor, or to straighten it so that the shoulders were aligned, the side seams hanging properly. Then she would slip her hands into each of the pockets. She did not hurry. She behaved as if this were an everyday activity, something that was moral, clean. She carried away distasteful items and disposed of them in the large waste cans by the exits. And today she passed a heavy, smooth bracelet into her purse and felt a sharp sting of satisfaction.

Evelyn knew that the bracelet belonged to Jill Adams, a student enrolled, but rarely present, in her 19th-century European history course. She remembered the jacket from the early, darker days of the term. On some of those days Jill Adams had sat toward the front of the classroom without taking off this crimson jacket, against which her dark curls had looked burnished. The bracelet Evelyn found surprised her—heavy and brass, with a jagged, asymmetrical edge that she found deeply pleasing.

Evelyn would never have said that it was a bracelet she was particularly searching for in students' pockets, but as she looked down at her wrist and felt the metal cuff bite into the back of her hand, she was warm with seamless, liquid pleasure. "Now," she said, addressing the three dogs impartially, "I must look for something to accompany this."

It took a long while. As the term rolled forward into heavy, sweet days and mild evenings that smelled of jasmine, the students left off their coats, left off sensible cardigan sweaters even on mornings that were still, in April, damp and keen. They came to Evelyn's classes—the ones who did come—in light dresses and shorts, their bare feet shoved into scuffed athletic shoes. Strolling through the student lounge at lunchtime, all she saw beside recently vacated seats were pyramids of texts and notebooks—piles that grew as the semester moved ponderously toward final examinations. She turned the bracelet that she wore sometimes, secretly, under the cuff of her blouse, and tried to hone her eyes, all her senses.

Since she had taken the bracelet she had felt heightened, as if she were filled with brilliant, flickering light. She could feel herself crackle in the mornings when she awakened and tossed back the covers, upsetting the five animals who had slipped in to share the room with her during the night. Her life was suddenly thrilling. What had once been pure order had become defiance, and as Evelyn tended to her pets, as she stripped down her storm windows and replaced them with screens, as she shopped in her prudent way for laundry detergent and beef liver, it whipped through her: She was now a woman who took things. She felt bold and daring, and when the cashier at the supermarket asked if she needed help with her groceries, Evelyn threw back her head and laughed, aware that she was flashing her sharp teeth.

She did not fear detection. That a hand might clap itself over her shoulder, some rough voice—she toyed with the ideas for the instant of alarm she could spark, nothing more. She was safe beyond imagining. That she, a fifty-three-year-old and respected professor of Locke and Hume might have endangered reputation and career for a bangle: It was ludicrous. And knowing this, Evelyn felt safe to prowl the union building, the snack bars and open-air concession stands, even the public restrooms across the university, craving some item that would restore the humming, startled brilliance that she felt slipping away from her fingers' furthest reach.

In the classroom her eyes searched as she lectured. She began to pace as she spoke, which she had never done. Her eyes passed briefly over every student, looking for pockets, parcels—places where anything she might desire could be hidden. She willed students to leave behind things that she could, strolling by, slip into her own pocket. Anything, she began to think. A candy bar, a notebook. But the students left her nothing.

Jill Adams continued to attend sporadically. Evelyn made a point of smiling at her when she came, and on the occasions she asked questions of the class, she looked invitingly at the student. But Jill Adams sat quietly, industriously taking notes, smiling at other students and gazing at Evelyn as if she'd never lost anything in her life.

At first Evelyn was troubled by this, but before long she was enraged. The young woman carried on as if nothing in her life had changed, as if the world were still the charmed place her parents had brought her to, as if she opened her eyes each morning to a world kind and constant. Evelyn wouldn't stand for it. "Relativism!" she found herself shrilling as she strode behind the lectern. "Revolution! Such thoughts were revolutionary. The understanding that all men must take their fates into their own hands." Evelyn looked down again and saw Jill Adams carefully writing. "Nothing," she said to her from across the room, "will necessarily bear out what people imagine themselves born to." Jill Adams wrote that too, and turned her gently molded face back to Evelyn. "Do you agree, Miss Adams?" she asked, feeling herself teetering on the brink of triumph.

Startled, Jill Adams blinked. Evelyn kept her gaze unswerving. "Do you agree?" she repeated, aware that she was bearing down, that other students were frowning as if she were imposing injustice of grand measure. "Have we the right to assume guarantees? Are there in fact birthrights? Inheritances of any kind?" She wished she were wearing the bracelet. She stepped closer.

Jill Adams trailed her fingers through her hair, then tossed it over her shoulder. She bit her lip and said, "How can you expect me to know that? I'm only nineteen." There was a groundswell murmur around her that in other circumstances, other quarters, could have sounded threatening. "I'm still trying to find things out," she said, or might have said—over the muttering of the class it was difficult to distinguish. And so, unexpectedly, it was Evelyn who at the end of the hour gathered her notes in an untidy bundle and was the first to hasten out of the classroom. Her forehead was damp and her clenched hands twisted as if to strangle or tear things, although all she grasped was air.

She hurried across the commons, clutching at papers as they slid from under her arms. She had managed, in the classroom, to keep herself from leveling a look at the woman, from saying, ''You are not immune,'' but the words were clanging inside her mouth.

She set her jaw and entered the lounge from the nearest door, dropping her things as the students did on the carpet near the dark fireplace. Upon straightening, she saw the nest of jackets and sweatshirts on the sofa before her—perhaps belonging to students who came from far out of town, who would take the early morning chill seriously. Moving abruptly slower, feeling each pulse like a slight blow, Evelyn went to the jackets and straightened them one at a time, gently, like a mother. She carefully folded the athletic jacket, the two windbreakers, the one goosedown vest that was cool and full against her hands. When she returned to straighten her own things, she slipped the watch unobtrusively into her pocket, and when she went to get a cup of coffee, she felt renewed, so clean and giddy it was all she could do to keep her feet on the ground.

She showed the timepiece to her pets three evenings later, held it out for the damp breath of her dogs, who were seated obediently in a row before her, and for the delicate noses of her cats. ''You see how heavy it is,'' she said. ''This would ordinarily be considered a man's watch. This is the mechanism,'' she pointed, and the dogs' wet nostrils flared and twitched, ''that opens the case. It allows us to view the workings of the watch.'' Evelyn looked down in satisfaction at the intricately locked bits of metal, the sharp and toothed cogs. ''One must be careful not to leave the watch open for long periods, since the smallest particles of dust can cause malfunction. But it is a pleasure, from time to time, to look at a well-crafted piece of machinery.'' The dogs, all three of them, wagged their tails. The yellow one woofed quietly. With some reluctance Evelyn snapped the watch case shut and stood.

She was wearing the bracelet again; she had come to like its heavy weight on her wrist when she took the dogs out. She hadn't yet decided what she would do if she were to run into Jill Adams on one of these walks—it was not entirely unlikely, in this small city. She frequently saw current and former students here, their glances darting and cool. It felt to her cowardly to plunge her hand into a pocket and mutter a downcast greeting. She longed to brandish the heavy brass coil before the girl, to display it on her ropy, hairless arm under a clenched fist. "You didn't suppose, did you? Can scarcely dream of the things you have lost." Engrossed in her thoughts, Evelyn let the dogs tumble out the front door without even the appearance of the discipline she usually tried to append.

By now she also knew who the watch belonged to. His name was Mark Harrison, he had been a student of hers in the prior term. She had read his description of the watch in the Lost & Found section of the student newspaper, and had experienced a tiny, exciting chill streaking up her spine. Reward, the notice had said simply.

Evelyn remembered Mark. A large boy with a gentle demeanor, he had sat near the front of the classroom and watched her with faintly worried eyes. He had had a troubled air—in her memory, he reminded her of some mournful, cautious animal, a hound or raccoon. He had never asked questions in class, but twice he had come to see her in her office, startling her on each instance. "How could those philosophers have expected ordinary people to reshape the world?" he'd asked her, his forehead rumpled. He had been a good student. It pleased Evelyn to have his pocket watch.

The dogs were tugging at their leashes so hard that Evelyn was veering acutely to the left; she gave a sharp snap, and they slouched back onto the sidewalk. With the watch to accompany the bracelet she felt securely planted in the world. It was not just a fluke, the impulse of a moment. The order of her life had opened up like huge jaws, and already she was aware that she needed to buy brass polish, must remember each night to gently wind the mechanism, taking care with its delicate old metal. (Old. She had learned that from the Lost & Found notice too. Antique, it had said. Heirloom.)

She felt blood pounding up hard under the tight skin of her face, drumming and boiling inside her body. The dogs were straining again, intent and urgent, on the path of a squirrel or chipmunk. She stood, twirling the bracelet on her arm and watching their claws eat into the soft earth. They were ripping up whole wedges of moist and sparse new grass, digging frantic trenches, slowly burrowing into the earth. "If I continue to stand here, will you dig until you hang yourselves?" asked Evelyn. They didn't so much as glance back at her. She had to call them twice, the second time so sharply that they slunk back to her as one penitent body, casting reluctant looks back up into the tree's wavering branches.

They continued to walk, past gardens packed with jubilant spring flowers, the sweetness rising from the hyacinths enough, Evelyn thought, to make a person slam to a halt, make her swallow. It was enough to make the blood rise and crest. The dogs were pulling hard in three directions, and for the first time that afternoon Evelyn watched them, seeing their nostrils flare and their ears rock back and forth, gathering in all the torrential richness of the spring air. She flared her own nostrils experimentally, and new air streamed into her lungs until she was dazzled.

She wanted to pound the softest flesh of her body against stone and sand for the pure pleasure of touch, to rub her face against bark like a cat. She wanted to scrape herself raw, drop blood in the damp soil. She was of the world, and she yearned to race with her pets back to the foot of the tree where they had dug, where they had turned back dirt like a blanket. She wanted to paw with them through the sweet loam and toss it back over her shoulders in a careless black shower. To go down until she was shoulder deep, deeper. Digging was the way to find treasures, and she had found she wanted all the treasures in the world.

When Evelyn happened to cross paths with Mark Harrison two days later on her way to class, she smiled at him. She felt that they shared a secret, something intimate and lovely. She had her hand on his watch, and felt it ticking in her fingers. He looked startled when she called his name, but he bobbed his head and managed to smile back at her.

"Are you happy this semester?" she asked him. What was she thinking? Foolish, impossible question—she, who'd taught that happiness was illusory.

"Excuse me?" he said.

"Happy. This semester." He gazed at her with his worried eyes, and she waved her hands about her shoulders. "The spring, you know. Revitalization."

"Ah," he said. "No."

No? She looked at him, his tender face still so young it bore hardly a mark—a boy was all he was. What reason could the world have to treat this boy harshly? "Why not?"

"Excuse me?"

He thought she had no right, but she did, she had the intimacy of ownership—heirloom, he himself had written. Flesh of his flesh. Reward. She had every right. "Why aren't you revitalized?"

His smile was crooked and uneasy. His ears flamed. "Just—a hard time. Setbacks. You know."

Evelyn was nodding, she did indeed. She would help him. Her whole life had been setbacks, but see! she had emerged. She had the nearly irresistible urge to take him by the wrist, lead him outside where they might sit and she could explain to him the things she knew. But he had shifted his weight back, was moving away from her. "I'm going to be late," he was saying, and "Have a nice summer," and she stood with her hand extended lightly before her as she watched him hurry away. This was the morning before Evelyn took the pen.

It had been lying in plain view beside some untidy papers; Evelyn had only had to sway a moment to pocket it, and the movement felt graceful, as simple as desire. The pen was what collectors called "a writing instrument"—heavy and full between her fingers, with an old-fashioned barrel for ink. Its nib narrowed to a point of such tense delicacy that Evelyn could hear as well as see the ink flow when she returned to her office and made cross-hatch marks across her blotter; the metal scraped with a tiny rush, like the sound of hummingbirds' feet. Across the body of the pen, in old Palmer Method cursive, was the owner's name, Susanna Moody. The present owner, or her grandmother? Evelyn knew herself to be no judge of such things, despite the generations of students whom she had judged and dismissed. Perhaps she had taught this very student, this Susanna Moody, she reflected, changing the angle of her hand so that the flow of ink became even finer. Perhaps she had received examinations written with this pen, attempting to interpret the importance of the German philosophers whose visions had risen, grand and terrifying, from a fearless life of solid morals and well-tended ledgers.

But as Evelyn looked at the pen, she knew. She had seen the hand-writing of young ladies at the beginning of the century. It was elaborate; it curled and swept like wings. Susanna Moody, that grandmother, had known how to use a writing instrument in a way that this careless girl who carried her name could not hope to appreciate.

There was a knock at the door—tentative, a student. "Yes," murmured Evelyn. There was a long pause, and Evelyn turned back to the pen, admiring its dull glow under the fluorescent light. Then the knock came again, even fainter, as if the student had moved back a step. "Yes!" Evelyn barked, and the door flew open.

It was a young woman, pale and fleshy, from the morning class. She looked at Evelyn and licked her lips. "I—" she said. Her eyes were round and dilated, her nostrils flared.

"What?" said Evelyn.

"I—" said the student. She was blinking rapidly.

"You have one minute," Evelyn told her. "I am busy; this is the place I come to do my work." Her hand lay easily and protectively over the pen.

"I want to study abroad," the student blurted. "I want to go to Germany. To go where Nietzsche was. And Kant. Everything you've taught me. It keeps me up at nights. You do, I mean. Your class, and revolution. I need your recommendation." She was still standing in the doorway, swaying slightly.

"How can I write you a recommendation?" Evelyn asked. "I don't even know your name."

The student, already colorless, became ghastly. She opened and closed her mouth silently, as if Evelyn had slapped her. She stood, her mouth working, for a minute, more. Then she turned to leave. When she closed the door she closed it softly and with elaborate care. Evelyn listened for the click of the handle, that precise and satisfying sound.

She practiced writing. She wrote a recipe for bread she had once learned: five pounds of flour, six cups of water, a package of yeast, salt. She wrote, Workers of the world, arise! You have nothing to lose but your chains! She wrote, Susanna Moody, and then she wrote her own name, Evelyn Mortimer, again and again in a staggering column to the bottom of her blotter. She was inept with the pen; ink spurted and strained, and her index finger was stained deep blue. It was evidence such as this, she reminded herself, that led to the capture of incautious thieves, or those simply lacking foresight. Evelyn locked the pen in her desk when she went to the restroom to wash her hand, and took care when she placed it in her purse. She laid it gently in a zippered compartment by itself, where it couldn't be scratched or jarred by the plastic ballpoints, the pins and check-book and pencil sharpener that filled the handbag. Then, after pack-ing the pen tenderly away, Evelyn locked her office door, rode the elevator to the ground floor, and sailed down the white granite steps of the building into the broad afternoon light.

Fifty yards behind Evelyn's house, its back wall defining the limit of her property, stood a cottage-sized dwelling. It had been a major selling point in the eyes of the realtor who had acquired the house for Evelyn; she had never tired of pointing out its potential as a guest house, a studio, a rental property. Evelyn had barely listened, her eyes lighting instead on the fenced-in yard and generous oaks whose trunks would stand up to any amount of clawing. Still, now she would be the first to admit that the house had its uses. When her sister Michelle had come to introduce her baby boy to Evelyn, the two had stayed there, and Michelle said she was perfectly content— "Just baby and me. We could stay here forever." They stayed until the boy took sick, and when Michelle took him back on the plane she had him swathed in a dainty yellow blanket so that Evelyn could see no child in her arms when she walked away.

She had become accustomed to neighbors, or at least the com-panionable sound of a household at the other end of the yard, and so after they left Evelyn sought out a new tenant, a woman who taught drawing in grade-school classrooms around the city. She had liked to cross the yard to Evelyn's back door, bringing pots of tea and biscuits for the dogs and samples of the brightly colored drawings her students—her children, she said—had completed for her that week. Red was always a featured color, Evelyn pointed out. Sally, the teacher, had laughed. "Do you suppose it's something terribly morbid? Do you think it's all that TV?" She laughed and laughed.

People had used to come to see her—men, on Friday and Saturday nights, arrived and helped her into their lustrous cars. Evelyn watched as night after night the teacher tossed back her head and laughed. She dreamed of the woman laughing. In her dream the art teacher laughed endlessly, some kind of unstoppable visionary laughter. She laughed until she gasped and held herself. She staggered, wiped her eyes, screamed with mirth. Her mouth was shapeless with her laughing. She laughed until fine seams appeared all over her skin like the crazed ceramic of her teapot. Then, all at once, the seams ruptured, her skin slipping off like a silky garment, leaving the flayed woman screaming. In her dream Evelyn watched all of this.

By day Evelyn was quick to appreciate the woman's good points; she was kind, and tidy, and never a day late with her rent payment. But in June, at the end of the school year, she told Evelyn that she wouldn't be renewing the contract. "I have other arrangements," she said and smiled in a way that Evelyn knew was inviting her to ask, congratulate.

"I'm sorry," Evelyn said. "You have certainly been a good tenant."

"Maybe," the other woman said, "you could come have dinner with us? I can show you my new place."

Evelyn looked down, unable to forget the woman, her skin sheared away. "Will there be another art teacher? Who will need a place to stay?"

The day she moved out Evelyn followed her through the house, noting repairs and replacements. She saw then a stack of foolscap in the bedroom, in a corner of the closet, and although she knew she should point it out to the art teacher, she said nothing. A stack of paper, untouched and clean, that would only smell like dust and aging as the years passed. Evelyn closed the closet doors and followed the young woman to the next room.

Less than a year later Evelyn received an announcement that the art teacher had given birth to a boy, Jason Michael. The card was whimsical, drawn in red crayon. Evelyn sent a note by return mail conveying her best wishes and lived delicately for some time after that, awaiting a phone call, a note of invitation. After a month

Evelyn called in painters to whiten all the rooms of the untenanted house. A woman came once a month to sweep and dust the baseboards, every three months to wash the windows. Evelyn hadn't been in the house since the painters left. Until this night, she'd half forgotten the house was there.

Now, the dogs skittering through the empty rooms and the pen in her pocket, she found the paper undisturbed, only the edges of the top sheets cracked and darkened. She ran her fingers over it, the pages smooth. It would serve her purposes, sheet after sheet of creamy, coarse-grained paper.

Still Evelyn did not leave the small house. It had been some months since she had been in it, close to a year. Clasping the foolscap to her chest, she wandered through the clean, empty rooms, the dogs clicking noisily behind her. The cleaning woman did her job well; the bare walls and floor shone. It was a shame that such a house should remain unoccupied, but Evelyn was reluctant to lose such perfect rooms. She remembered when her sister had stayed, and could hear still the baby's delicate, fretful wail.

Instead of returning to her own house, she spread the first page on the floor of the empty kitchen. The cats crouched at the edge of the paper, watching her and twitching their dark tails. The only way Evelyn could work was to stretch out on the floor, but she didn't hesitate—she was happy now, excited as a girl when she picked up the pen and began to trace words in large and stately letters. She practiced, making small notations, drawing musical notes and Greek letters. Then she wrote: A STITCH IN TIME SAVES NINE. She wrote: WE HOLD THESE TRUTHS TO BE SELF-EVIDENT. As she was crossing the final T, the male cat leaped across the paper to pounce on her moving hand, making the pen stutter across the page. Without a word she backhanded the cat across the kitchen, hard enough that she heard his solid impact against the refrigerator. He scrambled out of the room and she wrote: A FOOLISH CONSISTENCY IS THE HOBGOBLIN OF LITTLE MINDS.

She wrote: WE ARE SUCH STUFF AS DREAMS ARE MADE ON.

She wrote: SUSANNA MOODY.

She wrote: ALL THAT IS SOLID MELTS INTO AIR.

She wrote: DR. EVELYN MORTIMER. EVELYN MORTIMER. PROFESSOR EVELYN MORTIMER. She wrote with sweeping strokes that consumed the whole length of the oversized sheets. EVELYN, she wrote. EVELYN MORTIMER. Page after page, her body tingling. EVELYN MORTIMER, name bold, grand, EVELYN MORTIMER, she wrote, CONTAINS ALL THE WEALTH OF THE WORLD. She bore down until the pen quivered in her hand and its tip ripped through the page. She was writing on the floor itself, EVELYN MORTIMER, her face close so that she could see when the frail old metal finally splayed under her pressure and the nib split precisely in half, the ink puddling immediately on the clean floor. Then Evelyn stopped, dropping the pen, seeing how the metal had pulled back into symmetrical curls.

Ink was draining. If Evelyn didn't hurry, she would have to spend hours scrubbing at the blue stain on her floor. Instead, she picked up the edge of the paper, tipped it so that the ink ran across the page. She gently lifted the pen and brushed across the paper with generous strokes, the ink running in wide and graceful curves. She let it flow over her careful lettering, obscuring her labors, until the barrel ran dry and the page was dark and glistening. Then, as carefully, Evelyn laid her cheek to the page and slept. Her animals crept in to join her, padding into the wet ink until their prints, like the letters and shapes she had made, dried onto the white paper and floor and skin of the sleeping woman.

The next morning Evelyn went back to her own house and phoned the department secretary, telling her, as she never before had done, that she was too ill to teach her courses that day. The secretary was surprised and solicitous, offering to bring Evelyn medications, papers, whatever she might need. "No," Evelyn said. "I'm sure all that I need is rest." It was not entirely untrue; it was like a sickness, what she had.

When she had awakened in the cottage, the incandescent kitchen light still blazing and the animals, their fur gummed stiff with dried ink, wreathed around her, she had first groped for the pen. Gazing at the destroyed nib, its two halves flaring up like wings, she felt remorse so great her body shook. She spent the entire morning on her hands and knees in the kitchen, scrubbing again and again at the porous white surface, wringing out rags in diluted bleach until she could peel back the skin around her fingernails.

After two hours, she succeeded in obliterating the wide stain. With some difficulty she got to her feet again and made her way back to her own house, where two of the dogs were companionably chewing opposite ends of the ruined pen. Evelyn's hand came up. But instead of disciplining them, she bent to pick up the pen; there was little left of its graceful balance, and Susanna Moody's name was gone. Evelyn laid it on the arm of the sofa and went to get the dogs' leashes. From the closet she heard light metal scooting across the floor, the rustle and thump of a cat pouncing.

It was just past noon, a time Evelyn had never walked the dogs. Normally she would now be in the student lounge. For an unguarded moment she even considered taking the dogs there, seeing what they might find. Instead, she let them lead her. They were curious and happy, darting in different directions at once, tangling their leashes. She tried again to sniff the air as they did, but all she could smell was the caustic bleach on her own hands.

The dogs swung wide, heading toward the park that bordered Evelyn's neighborhood. Even from three blocks away she could hear the sounds of children there, their voices shrill with alarm or glee. Of course—at midday, children would be at a park. Generally Evelyn resisted such a long walk, but today she let the dogs go where they wanted, tripping over each other, panting, all three tails beating against her legs.

The park was busy with children. These were the young ones, too young yet for school, decked out in bright overalls and snub-toed sneakers. They swarmed around the sand lots and the construction of tires and two-by-fours that dominated the park, their shrieks rising free as balloons. Evelyn watched as a tiny, weedy girl chased a chubby boy around and around a sapling—her long white legs, skinny as pencils, and his dimpled, quivering ones. But the dogs were straining, pulling her into a slow circumference of the park, toward the baseball diamond and away from the children. Evelyn looked back as they towed her away, less with any discernible yearning than with detachment; the children gave her something to look at. "The time of innocence is short, the lifetime of sorrows insupportable," she murmured.

The dogs were crossing again, running into each other and Evelyn and snarling the leashes so that she had to make them sit around her until she could work them free. "Now just please go *straight,*" she said, and looked up to see, ten feet away, a baby. It was lying in a plastic carrier, wearing a yellow sleeper. It looked evenly at Evelyn until one of the dogs went to sniff at its cheek. The baby emitted a single squeal—pleasure? fright?—but made no other noise, not even when the dog licked its face uninterestedly and turned away.

"Oh," came a woman's voice behind Evelyn. "Oh. Don't let her bother you. She likes dogs." The woman came striding up, smiling. Her hair was tousled into an unbecoming ring around her face, and her eyes were so deep-set they were nearly invisible. "She likes coming here because she can see dogs."

Evelyn could see no evidence from the child that it liked anything. It lay still, looking not so much content as indifferent.

"Listen," the mother was saying. "Listen. I need to go over and check on the others—I'm block mother this week. Could you just stay with her here? Just for a minute? I'll be right back." She was ineffectually smoothing her hair back, smiling and nodding at Evelyn. Encouraging her.

"Of course," Evelyn smiled and nodded back. "I would be happy to." She wondered what a block mother was as the woman smiled again, then turned and strode back across the diamond toward the sandboxes.

The baby had the coolest gaze Evelyn had ever seen, as clean and level as smooth metal. She felt as if she were being watched by one not inclined to judge her lightly. So when she went to the baby and said, "Hello," it was no surprise that it began to scream in a voice that scalded by its clean volume.

"Hush now," Evelyn said. "Hush. You mustn't." She looked around, but there was no sign of the baby's mother. "You mustn't make such noise; it can't be good for you." The baby wailed. There were no tears, it didn't thrash about in its carrier, simply opened its mouth and bellowed until Evelyn chided herself for not carrying some bright object to distract a baby. The dogs were tugging at

Evelyn's wrist, anxious to get away; she had to fight to keep her balance. "Look," she finally said, pulling off the bracelet. "*Look.*" She held it before the baby's eyes, seeing the dull shine of the brass, how simple and lovely the line was, and seeing that this was no baby toy. Nevertheless, the baby reached for the bracelet, its cries cut as if a switch had been thrown.

It held the heavy circlet in both hands, turned it around and around, looking at it as carefully as an appraiser. "Well, what do you think?" Evelyn asked. It put the bracelet up to its mouth, rubbing its pink lips against the edge. "You like that? Well, I do too. We seem to share an appreciation for simple jewelry." The baby's hand wandered to the side of its head, where it tried to hang the bracelet on its ear. "Presumably you have not yet progressed to the learning stage of personal decor," Evelyn said.

The dogs were pulling again, and Evelyn stood, shading her eyes. "Are you really supposed to be here, in such sun?" she asked, looking down at the baby. "Babies are sensitive to the sun, you know, and prone to illness." The baby, fitting the bracelet over its nose and mouth, watched Evelyn silently.

"I know what will happen," she said. "If I try to take back the bracelet from you—my own property, or at least mine by right more clear than yours—you will begin to shriek again. If I walk away I shall feel guilty and look worse, if I take you with me I shall be accused of kidnapping by your mother, who is doubtless watching from the shrubberies. Do you really expect me to leave my bracelet with you through such transparent blackmail?" The baby looked at her.

"I have other things too that you might like," Evelyn said after a pause. "Scraps of metal. And a lovely watch—an heirloom. A very nice house with a large yard, and a guest house behind. A baby stayed there once before; it's a good house for babies. A good house for keeping things that the world gives us." She was squatting again, next to the carrier. The dogs were lying watchfully around her, their heads resting on their paws.

"There are such inequities—you might as well begin learning this at once. People will tell you that you outgrow desires, but they're wrong. We'll both want that bracelet just as much in thirty years. Things get away from us. All the promises are broken. We aren't meant, we never were, to live alone,'' Evelyn said, bending close, putting her face against the baby's. ''Never. You'll see that. We'll go to my house. I'll let you see things that I have now, that you'll like. I'll draw your name in red crayon; I'll write 'Susanna Moody' in red crayon on every wall of the house.''

Evelyn stood again and looked around her. All the people she saw were at the far end of the park, by the swings, the sand and tires. She found the handle of the baby carrier and lifted it, the baby contentedly running its tiny finger over the edge of the bracelet. The dogs, for once, walked in quiet formation before her. Evelyn looked down at the child and waited for it, the wave of exhilaration that would come crashing down on her with the force of a lifetime, the weight of everything she had ever been made to learn.

Tule Fogs

When Mary came back to Yuba City, the only available job for her was at the rectory. It wasn't a good job; the pay was low and she was uneasy moving carefully through priests' rooms, but she had no option—she had no money. Her mother looked up at her when she came home. "Next week," Mary told her; the priests had agreed to pay her every Friday until she was on her feet.

The job as they outlined it wasn't difficult. She was responsible for keeping the parish calendar and making Father Tomas' and Father Steve's appointments. She would see to it that the schedules of choir and school and sacraments meshed. She was to remind the fathers when it was time to visit other churches, the bedridden, prisons, and she scheduled meetings with the wealthy and well placed in the parish. She typed the weekly bulletin and the reports to the diocese. "It's not just a job you do here," Father Tomas told her the first day. "You work on the same side as the angels." Then he winked heavily at her and she managed to smile, although she had very little interest in angels.

It took only a day for word to spread across town that she was back and working for the parish. When she went home her mother told her that people had been calling for her—boys, she said, had phoned all day long. "I told them you were at the church."

"Nobody called," Mary said, turning her back and unbuttoning her blouse.

Father Steve watched Mary. He thought she needed someone to take her under wing; she was thin, and looked as if she would bruise at the lightest touch. They had never had such a young woman working there; it was impossible for him to walk past the small office without looking at her as she pounded on the old Olympic. He began to save little jokes for her because her smile, sulky as it was, seemed to him better than the blankness that usually settled across her face. He prayed for her with special fervor. Sometimes he daydreamed that he would go to her and talk, ask what it was that had damaged her, and he daydreamed that she would tell him.

Had she been from any other family, Father Steve could have gone to her mother. Most of the parishioners had lived in the Sacramento Valley for generations; they were people who called on priests, to sanctify their wide fields, to bless their children. They brought the first lettuce and cucumbers to the parish house every May, vegetables full of sweetness and moisture that could otherwise scarcely be found in that valley. They were people who knew each other, because there could be no secrets across fields where a man had to bend down to gather his harvests.

But Mary and her mother had never had anything to do with the land. Mary's mother had worked at the diner as long as Father Steve had been in Yuba City. She was listed as a member of the parish, but he had never seen her outside of the diner where, in the greasy air and the shiny uniform, she looked remote and beautiful. She had little to do with customers. She served them with efficiency and silence, and it was no secret that truckers coming from Modesto and Salinas would pass through Yuba City to look at Mary's mother while she gave them coffee and pie.

Mary lacked her mother's lush, flaring beauty, but she had all of her mother's sternness and precision of movement, and she had learned how to look at men flatly, without invitation. Father Steve could only guess at what Mary had done when she left Yuba City for Sacramento, and what had brought her back again. He began to ask her once, complimenting her on her efficiency in working through the tangle of records and ledgers. "Whatever it is that brought you back, it's a blessing to us," he said.

She met his smile with eyes flat as a goat's. "You will have eight o'clock Mass next week," she told him.

Mary had been taught to look for autumn in the sky first. Days still dawned early and hot, but the broad sky began to come blue again, tingeing the blank, baked white of the summer days. There would be more color every morning until the fogs came.

Farmers were beginning to calculate harvests. The trucks would be coming soon, and the migrants. Once, earlier, Mary had thought she would work in the fields during the harvest, earn her keep there as she had before she'd left. "You don't learn, do you?" her mother said. "They don't even speak English. Not that you need to talk, for what you do. You don't even need names." So she had waited. Impossible, though, to be in the town and unaware of the quickening in the fields on all sides, of the daily deepening of the hot blue sky.

The boys were calling Mary. Her mother didn't take messages for her, and Mary didn't ask. She had cut back; she saw only the rooms she shared with her mother, the bright, dusty walk to the rectory. She saw how her shadow, which had been full and round when she left Yuba City, had dwindled.

The first week she gave her mother seventy-five dollars. Her mother stood before Mary, her long palm still extended. "How do you plan to spend it?" she asked. "Makeup? You owe me." Mary gave her the rest of the money, and when she went to bed, lay flat and still on the sheet.

The boys waited for her outside the boarding house and the rectory, they waited for her along the way. They all had long, straight legs, thin arms. They were all so glad to see her back again. After Mary closed the wooden rectory door they went to the diner and watched her mother, whose skin looked like pearl in the heated, fatty air.

Father Steve rejoiced in autumn in the valley. He looked forward to rising at dawn, to seeing the mornings blue and yellow, shot through with bands of pure light. People poured into town to work and he rode out to the fields with them, picking and talking and more than once delivering babies, baptizing them on the spot with water from the irrigation pipes. The people were a wonder to him, a blessing; they would stay until the Tule fogs came and filled the valley. Masses overflowed every day. Father Tomas preached against the fighting, the drinking, fornication in the soft nights, but to Father Steve the days seemed pure since color had returned. He preached rebirth.

He asked Mary to go with him into the fields and help him there. "No one told me I would have to go into the fields," she said. "No one said anything about that."

"You don't have to come," he said as gently as he could, thinking, *Slow. Slow down.* "It's pretty there now, you know. Nice. I thought a break from this office might do you good."

"I have to stay here. I have to unlock the church for the choir at three. There's CCD this afternoon. Father Tomas went to Marysville; who's going to answer the phone?"

He could see the planes of her shoulder blades through her white blouse. A man could trace the ridge of her spine with no pressure at all. "You're very devoted to us, Mary. We're fortunate."

She shrugged, her eyes still dull. When he went to the fields, the heat thick and noisy with flies, he imagined how she would look stepping between the rows of lettuce, her fingernails crammed with soil. He thought of her shoulders moving under her blouse as she cut the lacy heads from their stalks. The workers there grinned and called out to him, and toddlers stumbled over to hug his knees while he blessed them all. But the thought of Mary never left him that day, like a heavy scent that clings to everything it touches.

He had the five o'clock Mass that afternoon, and he came back into town with just enough time to wash before putting on the heavy vestments and throwing open every door of the church. When the time came for personal petitions, he prayed, as he always did, for the needs of the parish. But as he prayed he saw Mary, her face harsh and closed, and so he prayed for her, and for guidance in dealing with her mother.

Because he so loved to be in the fields in the blazing, crowded days, and because he was afraid to go to her home, Father Steve put off going to the diner; he waited for a rainy day that would force him indoors. But there came no sign of rain in the dusty air, and every day Mary seemed to retreat further, folding in on herself like a bird's wing. Father Tomas scarcely noticed—he passed through the rectory quickly before starting his circuit to the other towns. "It is sad; look how children today have no joy," was all he said. Father Steve

was left to note the progress of the blue shadows around Mary's jaw
and the inside of her wrists. Her flat eyes were beginning to glitter
across their surface, like the play of light on swampy, fetid water. He
went to her mother when he looked in the wastebasket under her
desk and found handfuls of hair.

At eleven in the morning the diner was quiet. Mary's mother
was wiping down the counter in long, calm strokes. She brought
him coffee without asking and checked on the two truckers eating
breakfast before she came back and met his eyes, her order pad
in hand.

"Can you talk for a few minutes?" he said.

"What do you have to talk about?" Flat eyes, like her daughter's.
But he had known that.

"I'm concerned about Mary. I don't think she's well." Not
enough, of course. Not what he needed to say.

"She's working all right?"

"She's a very hard worker. She's a blessing to us. But—" And
now he was completely at a loss. Looking at Mary's mother's mud-
colored eyes, and seeing too the shining, shining skin, the wealth of
hair and firm waist, he was afraid to say: She is lifeless. Or, she is
losing her life. "She's pulling out her hair."

"I know."

"It's not natural. For a girl her age."

"It's not that unnatural. She has plenty left. Is that the only
problem?"

He hadn't expected this, Mary's mother standing impatient next
to him. And so he hadn't expected to have to defend his own pity,
or think, *I'll make you care.* "You don't think something is
wrong?" he said. "You can't see that we're losing her? She's fading
every day. She's slipping right out of our hands." He could only say
all of this if he didn't look at Mary's mother, and so he focused on
the battered Orange Crush sign behind the cash register, the adver-
tised specials: patty melt, Coke. When he did look back at her
mother she was studying him with a thin smile.

"I don't know, Father, that you're the one that needs to worry
about losing her."

He began, wanted to say, *I am a priest.* "She's your daughter," he
said instead.

"I know all about her. There's nothing she does that I don't know about. So let me tell you not to worry about losing her—worry about losing all those Mexican babies. They deserve your worry. I can tell you we won't lose Mary. I can *promise* you."

So he left, slamming into the Falcon and driving far and fast, into Yolo County, past Davis and Winters and then east, into Sacramento and Folsom, fields giving way to rice and soybeans and then, finally, south of the city, lettuce again, and he ground his teeth and prayed through his clenched jaw that he be given patience, be shown the way, that the Lord help Mary, and her mother.

Mary kept enough money out of her paycheck to buy a pair of tweezers, and she was plucking the hairs from her legs and arms one at a time. There was a sharp, precise pain with each hair; she would inhale, blink, pluck another.

She did it in her room at night with the curtains drawn over the open windows. The boys were outside, waiting for her. She would never have imagined they could be so patient. "They come into the diner like dogs," her mother told her. "Business picked up when you came back."

Mary was working to streamline herself. When she brushed her hair at night she could feel how thin it had become, and she raked the bristles across her scalp, snagging and ripping the remaining strands. She used the bathroom at the rectory for pulling out her eyelashes, which slid out painlessly between her fingertips. With the tweezers she started removing her dark eyebrows, working from the outside toward the center of her face. Every day she looked blanker, like a moon. She was satisfied with her progress.

She knew that Father Steve was watching her. His heavy footsteps always slowed when he approached the office. Her mother told her he had come to the diner. She wore her sheerest white blouses, her tightest skirts, and watched the way his eyes came back to her. The boys had never looked at her; when they came they looked at each other, or the sky. They found her, she thought, by smell. But Father Steve looked at her every day, and she thought of him watching her in the mornings as she dressed. She was sure it would not be long before he came to rest his hand on her shoulder, before he began to touch her.

It seemed to Father Steve that everything rushed after his conversation with Mary's mother. The harvest was coming in too fast, more than any number of hands could keep up with, and the workers stayed in the fields until nine and ten o'clock, covering acre after acre, racing for the firm lettuce heads. Evening Masses were deserted again. The fogs would soon begin; it was only a few weeks before they would be there in earnest, muffling the town for days at a time and distorting all distance and sound. It was when the fogs came that Father Steve prayed with something like desperation, begging that God not desert His people and leave them struggling for breath in the white air.

He watched Mary work as if she were fevered. She raced through the typing and duplicating he gave her, she made phone calls and arranged meetings weeks in advance. She began to come to his study, asking if there wasn't more she could do. Father Steve looked at her and saw skin that was white in the season when faces were brown and chapped. She had plucked her eyebrows so fine and high that he could clearly see the ridge of bone above her eyes. She looked as if she came to him from another planet. And he carried the look of her bright, bald stare with him through the days and nights, remembering despite himself how tiny her wrists looked as she hammered at the old typewriter.

He didn't trust himself to go to her, even after her hair was half gone. He prayed for her instead, whenever he thought of her, daily, hourly, constantly. He imagined that he had seen the pulse jump in her throat, and it was an intimate thought. He spent long days in the fields with workers who silently made room for him; there was no time now for joking as they worked. One night he drove without explanation back into Sacramento, up and down all of the dark and featureless streets, wondering where she had been, what she might recognize if she were there on the car seat beside him. By the time he returned to Yuba City it was late, past midnight, and the house where Mary lived with her mother was dark. For the first time in many years Father Steve spent the night in a church, kneeling on the cool tiles, repeating the prayers of men who had known how to recognize temptation, and how to resist it, and how to find in it glory.

The next day dawned hot and blue, and Father Steve felt safe in his exhaustion. At least, he knew, he wouldn't be dazzled or weakened by the sharpness of the morning, when even the aloes and junipers were drenched in color. When he came back into the rectory he saw the boys there, standing restlessly around the door, and he blessed them. He moved through the day as if carried by some strong tide. Mary looked like a fledgling, and he smiled at her tenderly as he passed the office, thinking that it was just such that the Lord would hold to His bosom, just such that He had saved.

It was beginning again. Mary remembered it from the last time, how her mother began to work later at the diner and how she herself sat in her room in the dark, waiting for the boys to come. She remembered the sound of their feet on the hard dirt outside her window, their indistinguishable voices, the soft slap of hard skin on skin as they jostled for position. When they did call up to her, the voices rose like baying. She would have had it no other way. Knowing that her mother was at the bright diner serving the men who came to look, Mary turned on the light so the boys could find her.

Father Steve hadn't planned on going back to the diner. Mary's mother's scorn clung to him, and he didn't trust himself to rise above it. He had lost control—he wanted too much to make her see, to force her to look at her daughter. It was Father Tomas who finally told him to go, saying, "The child is not well. Has her mother been too busy to notice? It is our duty to tell her." Then he went to the diocesan meeting, leaving Father Steve in the dry night, the air cakey in his lungs. At seven he walked across town, remembering the bright, exultant look Mary wore at work lately, her face now only bone and taut white skin, her scalp visible under her remaining hair. He had no idea what he would say to her mother; he thought, *I will trust in the Lord.*

He slowed as he approached the diner. Half a dozen rigs were parked there, along with the battered pickups that brought in the help from the fields. Even across the street he could hear the tinny jukebox, and over it the clatter of cheap, heavy dishes. Father Steve could imagine the dishes passing through Mary's mother's hands,

envisioned without effort how cooly she moved through the noisy
room. He crossed the street and went not to the door of the diner but
to the window, where he could watch her.

It was dark enough by then to watch without being seen. There
were no empty seats, and men sat in booths and at the tables, behind
plates piled high with potatoes and steaks, watching Mary's mother.
Father Steve pulled himself up straight and looked directly in the
window—no one would see him there as long as they had her
mother to look at, lavishly beautiful in the loud, low-ceilinged
room. She moved easily, without hurry or extra motion, as if her
body were a single exquisite muscle. How could anyone, looking at
her, imagine her daughter's blue shadows and hairless eyes? She
should never have been allowed to have a daughter, he thought. The
Lord should never have permitted it. And he watched her balancing
and writing and calling in orders, the soft old fabric of her uniform
curving over her shoulders and hips like skin.

There was nothing—nothing—of Mary here. Father Steve gazed
at the mother and tried to think of the daughter, and when the image
of Mary came to him it was frighteningly small. He had planned to
tell her mother, *She sits at the desk and shakes. Quivers, really, is
what she does,* he had practiced on the way from the rectory. He
would have liked to say more, that her eyes had begun to spark and
flare, light enough from her eyes alone to awaken him from dreams,
and that he had begun to see the world in her measure—a branch no
wider than her ankle, clouds white as her inner arm.

His eyes didn't leave Mary's mother, and for a moment he imagined he was trapped there, bewitched: She knew, he thought briefly,
that he was there, and was performing for him on the well-lit floor
of the diner. He began to feel the rhythm of her movements, the
humming balance of her body as she swung from table to table, and
he was content to watch her so, even the scorn that lit her face, and
he thought of Salome, and the ease of those who watch, and for the
first time he looked at the others there watching her and thought, *We
want this.* It was then that he saw Mary again, searingly bright, and
he closed his eyes and steadied himself against the windowsill, his
vision full of her and his hearing full of the rhythm of his own pulse.

In Mary's room the boys were everywhere, watching and touching.

She would do anything to keep them there. She didn't mind that they talked about her mother. Tomorrow, yes, and days after that, and the nights when the white fog came and held the town, when her mother would walk home late from the diner and not see who might be waiting. Mary knew who watched her mother. She was keeping them from her.

Father Steve walked headlong through the warm air. He loosened his collar as he went, bent forward at the waist as if walking against a wind. He was going to Mary. When he came to her house he would take her with him, he would carry her if he had to, he would take her to a safe place and talk to her about love. He would wait until her pulse quieted, and he would hold her so that she could not touch her hair, and when she slept he would stroke the blue shadows of her white throat.

for WTS

The Punch-Up Man

Every night when he comes home he works to surprise us. I emerge from the kitchen to see him tumble in the front door, spring up to the end table and balance an ashtray on his nose. He handsprings across the front lawn ten minutes at a stretch, waiting for us to notice. If passersby stop to watch him—thirty-five years old and snapping like elastic across the yard—he pretends he doesn't see them. He trumpets my name—"Elena! Elena! Oh, I love her so"—until I come outside to him. He brings home puppets and jack-in-the-boxes, then he mugs and shuffles away when we thank him. "Aw. It was nothing."

In a flash he's back again, waltzing me willy-nilly down the length of the living room and turning to shadowbox the wall. The words come as fast as he can throw them. "Guy comes into a bar and the keep says, 'What'll it be?' Guy says, 'A bottle of Jack and directions to where I can find a good dog.' Too slow, too slow. 'Bottle of Jack and a dog.' That's punch." He's still throwing them, right, left, right, right. Our son, two feet below him, is punching too. His father says, "Girl comes in later, sees the dog, says, 'Who's your friend?' and guy says, 'Waldo. Any problems?' Girl says, 'No, just asking.' All wrong. Boring. Who knows where they get these scriptwriters. Girl should say, 'I had an uncle named Waldo.' Then cut to the dog sleeping on the guy's boot. *That's* punch." It is. We agree.

Our boy lives for his father's return every evening. I catch him practicing cartwheels and somersaults, his face buttoned up with concentration. When he sees me watching him, he breaks into his sunniest smile, the one he knows melts my heart, and he executes a tidy buck-and-wing that his father taught him. He doesn't talk much around the house with me, but his teachers tell me he has a way with words, a gift. His father's child. "My boy," my husband croons when he comes home at night, lifting him like nothing and whizzing him through the air. What can I say? This is strictly a father-and-son act.

"Listen to this, son," he'll say. "The script calls for two street vendors, one to sell the hot dog and one to pick the guy's pocket. Director doesn't like it. How come?"

"Too crowded," our son says promptly.

"What should they do instead?" asks my husband, the coach, the pedagogue.

"Have the vendor sell the dog and show him fingering the guy's wallet after he walks away," says our son. "Punch, punch."

My husband crows and beats out a flourish on the coffee table with his hands. He and my son come soft-shoeing into the kitchen to me and make a great show of picking my apron pocket and I, on cue, make a great show of laughing. My husband catches sight of his shadow against the yellowed wallpaper and jabs at it once, lightly.

My mother doesn't know about any of this. She thinks—I myself told her, what could I have been thinking of?—that my husband directs. I make up movies and tell her he was solely responsible: *Zaporetto,* an avant-garde western; *Nils Koeniger,* a film noir. So she asks me if he works with famous stars, when he's going to do a picture she's heard of. "I'd like once to see my artistic son-in-law's name on the screen." Who can blame her? My husband is very pleased with me for having given him this role. He wears a black beret when we go to my parents' house, he lurks around corners and squints through tiny frames he makes with his fingertips. My father never says anything, but he looks irritated when my husband comes lurking around. I try to keep our boy out of his way. I think my father's onto them.

When our son was born I suggested that my husband tell my father everything. I thought it was time, or that it was one of those things that men would naturally understand, handed from father to son like an inheritance. A calling. I thought maybe it was like Elks,

Lions, Odd Fellows. My husband staggered across the hospital room, his hand over his heart. He backed to the corner, slid down the wall, then sprang across the room in a neat one-and-a-half to land on his knees by my bed, holding my hand. "Nope," he said.

He never has talked about it. When I went to his house the first time, before we were married, I asked my husband's father what he did. His wife, now my mother-in-law, reached out to restrain him, but it was too late, he and his son, now my husband, were at it, tapping happily around the dining room table. "We're just a couple of song and dance men," they sang, father and son. "I'm the song," sang the father. "And I'm the dance," sang the son.

His father sashayed to the china cupboard and pulled out a tall stack of plates. He began tossing them to his son, who juggled them as they came, occasionally fancying things up by catching under his leg or behind his back. Neither of them missed a beat.

"Who's buried in Grant's Tomb?"

"Why did the chicken cross the road?"

"Other than that, Mrs. Lincoln," they chorused, "how did you like the play?"

"See, it's the way you say 'em," his father said to me as he came back to the table. His son started to follow him, then rushed back into the center of the room just in time to catch the plates as they came raining down.

"Punch," he said, handing them lightly back to his father.

"Punch, punch," his father feinted after handing off the plates to his mother. They sparred around the table as the roast settled and cooled, and his mother and I watched them, the plates safe on her lap. I think, looking back, that she was smiling, but who could know? Son and father, they were around the table quick and light as dragonflies, and I couldn't wait for him to propose—the son, the father, someone; I was losing track.

Soon after we were married my husband started bringing home photos taken at the dailies showing him with his arms around glamorous and powerful men and women. He would drop them in my lap as he cha-cha'd by, and when I asked him what he wanted me to do with them he looked at me with a loose smile and a shrug. "They're all yours, sweetheart," he would slur, segueing into an elegant

foxtrot across the carpet. "I can't give you anything but love.
Scooby-dooby-doo." They wound up anywhere, under the bed and
in the placemat drawer and in between towels. You lose track of that
kind of thing after a while.

My husband has somewhere all the photos of his father standing
with Zanuck and Griffith, and with the anxious-looking men who
my husband tells me were the studio screenwriters, the hacks. He
has albums full of them, along with signed stills from Myrna Loy,
Jean Harlow, Clark Gable. The only picture that he keeps out and
framed on our dresser doesn't show his father at all, just Sam Gold-
wyn's doughy face collapsing into a fist of laughter. "Dad used to
make him laugh," my husband says.

"What about your mother?" I have asked him. "What about her,
anyway? She had a hand in this."

"M is for the Many things she gave me; O is for her Oatmeal thick
as glue." He always drops to one knee, wherever we are—once, in
the parking lot at Safeway. "M is for the Milk of parturition; O is
for the Organ that she played."

"What would you say to her, if you saw her again? If you saw her
on the street?" He would have to be the one doing the talking; I've
forgotten her face, wouldn't know her if I saw her.

"Hey, you're beautiful, kid. Let's do lunch. No." He frowned a
moment, then smiled at me and took my hand. "This is, I believe,
our dance." He took me, the groceries, all of it into his arms and we
whirled across the parking lot.

My mother doesn't understand, and because she doesn't understand, she doesn't trust. "You're sure," she was still saying the
morning of our wedding. "You're sure? Because it isn't too late.
Know that. Even now, it is not too late. Everybody will understand." I straight-armed her out of the way, climbed into my white
dress. I couldn't understand why it was so hard for her to see. He
was the man of my dreams.

She came around some when our son was born; she'd despaired of
my marriage, my husband—but a grandchild! A grandchild she
could understand. "It's the show business," she used to tell me
knowledgeably, nodding in the direction of my husband. "It's in his
blood." Shameless, she would arrange to have friends stop by,

would clear room in front of the fireplace for our boy to display his
first time step or cramp roll—chubby knees pumping and pumping,
smile wide as a door. Showy, is what it was. He had us eating out
of his hand. My mother and her friends would smile and cluck, point
out how adorable he was. My husband would watch him from the
doorway in a raincoat and hat, his collar up and his brim down. My
father would snort and leave the room—before long we'd hear the
high whine of the electric saw coming from the basement. And me,
I'd whistle and clap, stamp my feet and tumble our son into my lap
after his final bow. Those days are long gone, though I imagine if I
tried I could still feel his gurgling weight on my lap. Now when we
go to my parents' he does stand-up comedy or magic tricks.

"Seems to me," I tell my husband every time we drive home,
"this marriage has done great things for my family. We never used
to know from entertainment."

"But now that the stars are in your eyes, I'm beginning to see the
light," he sometimes sings. Or, when he's tired, he settles: "Another op'ning, another show." A good husband, he always lets me
know how he's feeling.

"And we're just getting more entertaining all the time," I said the
last time, two weeks ago, as he drove us home. Our son was beating
out some complex, steady rhythm on the velour backseat.

"What is it that we're living for?" sang my husband. "Applause,
applause." This was a good sign—he was awake, listening carefully, making sure he was a step ahead of me. What I was trying to
do, what I've been trying to do for weeks now, was tell him that I'm
pregnant again. Much longer, and it won't be something I have to
tell him.

"Hard to believe that only three people can have so much," I
said. "Talent. Beauty."

"We've got elegance, if you ain't got elegance, you can never
ever carry it off."

"Elegance? We've got *genes*. We're a regular royal family."

"Duke, duke, duke, Duke of Earl, Earl, Earl," sang our son from
the back.

"Hardly seems fair, does it? That just the three of us can have so
much and everyone else—" I spread my palm and shrugged, "—so
little."

"Them that's got shall get, them that's not shall lose."

"I just wonder if we aren't being unfair. Don't we owe it to humanity to share the wealth?"

"I never promised you a rose garden," sang our son.

"Punch," said his father.

He was quiet. I stole a look in the rearview mirror and saw him looking down, frowning. His father hummed a few notes.

"Willing to try, to do it or die," our son sang immediately. His father joined him for the big razzmatazz chorus: "I've gotta be me." I let it drop.

But he knows that something's afoot all right, my husband does. He came home the next night in whiteface and tails and presented me, with a bow and a great flourish, a white paper cone. I held it carefully, knowing something would come—flowers, doves, billowing smoke. I put nothing past him. He stood and stared at the cone, his whole body slanted toward it, but while both of us waited it remained plain and still in my hands. Minutes went by. I glanced at my husband, but he was motionless, steadfast as a bird-dog. We were charged and crackling when he finally took it back from me with a monstrous frown. He peered into it and shook it and looked as if he would smash it on the floor. I caught his arm, of course, wrenched it back as he knew I would, and as I grabbed the cone it began tinkling "I've Got You Under My Skin." No question—he knows that there's something, and he will give me music boxes until the cows come home to keep me from telling him. It is, in fact, worse than he thinks, because I believe this baby is a girl.

Until now I've always been skeptical of these things, the mysterious wisdom that women smugly intuit. I've never had sudden, clear visions or any calm certainties about the future, I've never laid claim to extraordinary, private knowledge. It's upsetting to find myself in this position where I know, I simply know. More than that, it's embarrassing. I don't know how to behave or explain myself.

I've spent three days ransacking our house for my husband's mother's address. After his father passed on his mother left town; I remember we all said at the funeral she would stay with relatives, I remember we all agreed that it would be best, I remember more clearly than any of that how I couldn't stop looking at my father-in-law's impossibly solemn face in the casket. Now, too late, the guilt comes down on me like trees: to have lost track of my own mother-in-law. Not even to know if she's in the same state, not even to know if she's alive. And to know that it was so easy. I wonder if she forgot her own mother-in-law with such dispatch, only to find herself longing for some other female, a daughter, one of her own. I wonder how many times she looked at her son and thought with utter certainty: I had no hand in this.

I sat down with our son at lunch last week. "How are you feeling about school these days?" I asked him. What was I thinking of? We never talk like that.

"You say banana, I say banawna."

"Your teachers have lots of good things to say about you. They say you're quite a scholar."

"Anything you can do, I can do better."

"That's no answer." I longed, there at the table, for a son who couldn't sing, for a son who squirmed and shrugged and answered all questions with "Fine"—a son whose single clever comments I would savor and repeat on family holidays. "All I'm asking you for is a civil response. I don't really think that's asking so much."

"Punch," he said.

"That's no answer." Fingers raking over the formica, I was on the verge of screaming at my own child. And thinking even then that I should have said "That's not so much" because it would have been snappier, it would have had punch. *"That's no answer."* For a moment I thought I could feel the new one, the baby, kicking and hitting, though I knew it was far too early, and there I was thinking automatically what a good thing, kicking already, she'll be a hoofer.

My son sat still, watching as my fingernails scraped over the table. I couldn't think of a single thing to say to him, my clever boy, my star. I wondered what he would say if I asked him how he would like to have a little sister. "There is nothing like a dame," maybe. He could work out a little soft shoe over in front of the stove. I was already seeing long glides across the linoleum, shoulders angled, all elegance in the kitchen when he pushed his chair back, picked up his plate and put it in the sink, and quietly went out the back door, holding the screen so it didn't bang shut. He moved with perfect grace and avoided my eyes.

I didn't think anything. I didn't think he might be running away, or even going to his father at the studio. I didn't think of traffic or undertows or men who whisper soft words to pretty boys. When he came back into the kitchen five minutes later I was still in my chair, memorizing the floor's pattern and slope from stove to refrigerator. He stood looking at me with both hands hidden behind his back.

"That one," I said, pointing. He thrust his hand forward. It was a good-sized bouquet; he must have worked fast. There were geraniums and marguerites that he could have gotten from our yard, and there were four perfect white rosebuds that could only have come from our neighbors'. My son and I smiled at each other. "All we are saying," I sang tunelessly, "is give peace a chance."

"That's no answer," he told me.

The trouble is I don't know how to get an answer, how to make someone give me one. I try to be practical, but my mind goes out of control and skids away. Talking to my husband I forget myself, lose my words, and imagine him handspringing from our yard across the neighborhood, into the next county, far enough to send me postcards. How can I follow him? Me, broadening again, back and breasts aching—it's all I can do to walk to the post office and grocery. When I was carrying our son, my husband rubbed me down every night with lotions and oils he bought on the way home from work. He found one that he swore was myrrh—when he tipped the vial the fluid slipped out slow and thick as a drowsy snake—and our bedroom smelled like camels and honey for three days. A girl should come into the world that way, the scent of rich and potent oils in her nostrils.

"Were there ever any girls in your family?" I asked my husband.

"Must have been. Hard to account for me otherwise." He was playing with his hair in front of the mirror, twisting it up into little horns at his temples, then skinning it back tight from his face, like a ballerina.

"I wish you'd hurry up and get that cut. Weren't there ever any sisters? Did your father have any aunts?" Why stop with his father? It went back for generations. Even Shakespeare needed a little extra punch once in a while.

"We all take solemn vows: Any girl children are handed over at birth to MGM, and they emerge seventeen years later as starlets. Oh sure," he said airily, "Lana, Tuesday, Tippie—I call them all Sis."

"What about your mother?"

"I called her Sis, too."

"Didn't she ever want any other females around?"

"Dad was going to send her to the convent after I was born as tradition dictated, but in a magnanimous gesture that was loudly heralded on all sides, he kept her on for meals and light housework."

"Not funny."

"Punch?"

"Yes."

"Yes," he said. "She wanted other females."

"What did your father do?"

"Got her a rabbit," he said, combing his hair straight up on each side of his face, like tall ears.

"What would you do?"

"Get you whatever your heart desires."

It had to be enough. How much could I ask of the man? "She'll need dancing lessons, I suppose."

"Yes," he said gravely. "A rabbit doesn't go far in this world without dancing lessons." He hopped out of the bedroom, hair flopping down over his eyes.

He can't keep this up forever. One of these nights he'll come to sweep me off my feet and find me immovable, massy and unavoidable as Mount McKinley, and then surely we'll get down to business. We'll talk about names—his mother? mine?—and he'll begin thinking of new songs. What else can he do? We've made a stage with no exits or wings, nowhere to change for the next number.

I go through entire days holding hot and close and secret as a lover this idea: a daughter. After my son and husband leave I move slowly through the house, looking through windows at easy, ordinary things—trees and birds, cars, the ocean. I have to make sure she sees them now. I'm teaching her plain things and daily things. Things she'll need to keep her feet on the ground, like her mother's. These days I'm as stable as anything vast, grand pianos and woolly mammoths and expanses of rock as wide as continents.

Don't imagine that I don't know what I'm doing. I'm savoring her like chocolates. Lying in bed at night I fight to stay awake so I can remember how all day we looked at the world together, moved together, communicated over hot, wordless channels. I'm trying to burn these memories into our brains, the deep crevices where the things are kept that are never forgotten, because I know what's coming, I know perfectly well. At night, when my husband lies sleeping with his arm around me, I know it's sure as eggs. She'll love him. She'll see how he dances for her and sings. He'll come to her all dressed in gold and she'll never stand a chance.

I close my eyes and it plays in front of me like a feature presentation. There are she and her brother singing, there's her father teaching her the shuffles and turns and kick-ball-change. The words come soon and she learns them quickly. She waits at the window every evening as my son and I do; we watch for him, impatient for the show to begin. Every night the three of them shuffle and spin and high-step around the couch, and then the boys—my son, my husband—hold back, give her a solo. She's charming, dainty—she's America's sweetheart. And then it's their turn, and she drops to the back of the stage, over by the mantel. I can see her pretty smile as she watches them, and they're smooth as waves, juggling and singing and orating and leaping—all at once! It's a wonder. I can watch her as my son and husband flicker before us like firelight, and she can see me if she only looks. That's where I freeze it. Every night I drop off seeing the two of us, my girl and me, standing quiet while they, in the harmony of perfect understanding, are caught throwing punches for all they're worth.

Legs

Even years later, Paul Castle was able to remember the afternoon his mother called him about his aunt Frances. He liked to think that from the first mention of her coming, a jagged thrill had torn through him, a lightning stroke of apprehension and joy, but that was not the case. He had been at work, aggravated over registrations that had been done sloppily at the color lab. There were no clues—no swell of music, no change of lighting or focus. Nothing in the world to suggest that she would be the woman of his dreams.

"We're inheriting her," his mother said. "Sid and Helen can't manage any more, since Helen's stroke."

"Mmm," Paul said. He was squinting at the layout, groping with one hand for the color wheel.

"Sid says Frances doesn't say anything anymore, not even crazy things. She just doesn't talk. He's flying out with her next week."

At least the lab had gotten the colors right. It was a good cover, an interesting, jazzy balance. If Paul talked to the people there right away, they might still be able to have it ready on time. "So what are you going to do? Keep her with you?"

His mother sighed. "We have the address of a home. They say it's very nice." There was a silence, while Paul eyed the spacing on the heads. "It's such a shame. When you think about what she did, everything she knew."

"No regaining the past," Paul said, quoting his mother.

"But a person can wish," she said. "You never know."

Paul had never met his aunt Frances, his mother's oldest sister, but he had grown up in the fading illumination of her lore. She had been a starlet, a Busby Berkeley chorus girl who called herself Stella Sand. His mother couldn't quite remember any movie she had been in—Frances had left home when his mother was only five—but she remembered and told Paul about her sister who came home once in a narrow white gown, accompanied by a man with flashing teeth.

Perhaps it was because of this—a blood tie, a claim—that Paul spent his boyhood entranced with Hollywood. He rode his bicycle down the steep streets near Pickfair and Mary Astor's mansion, blistered and menacing as the roads were. The walls of his bedroom were dense with publicity stills from movies made twenty years before he was born.

He understood the throbbing prose of early fan magazines, girls fainting in the streets at openings. Movie stars shone high above the rest, they spun, movie after movie, into futures filled with light and life. It was an orderly world, it had patterns: Good prevailed, death was a valiant act, and when couples danced, they moved with silky grace. By the time Paul was ten, westerns came from Italy and love stories featured gangling, unattractive people; he fled to the revival houses to watch whole festivals of Fred Astaire.

Of course he had asked about his aunt. He badgered his mother and her other sisters for details. What movies had she been in? What years? But they couldn't remember now, she had been so vague for so long, and eventually he stopped asking. He expanded the photos to the ceiling, so that the collected beauty and heroism, an inch thick in places, held him apart from the world and the famously unclear Los Angeles sky.

When he was eighteen Paul went to art school. It seemed a reasonable choice; there he was able to paint the sinuous drape of Norma Shearer's evening gowns, sketch a hood ornament for a car, all legs and streaming hair. "Retro," his teachers said approvingly. "Good practice." But Paul wasn't practicing; making these long lines and full, erotic shapes he felt himself dwelling in the rich center of his life. He brought to the studio space his favorite photos, the best ones—Theda Bara, a young Marlene Dietrich, fashion shots of models whose flesh was pale and smooth. There was nothing in his world that could compare, and looking at the elegant forms that crowded his notebooks and walls, he felt his future like a brilliant field he needed only to step into.

Other students saturated huge canvases in auto paint, or shunned canvases altogether and created installations with bare walls and neon. They set out to make statements. Glancing at his drafting board, another student named Falcon said, "That's been *done*. Why don't you try something new?"

Because no one is doing this now, he wanted to say, because everything had become jumbled and awkward and defiant, and because the loss daily rang through him. "It's in my blood," he told her, and abruptly realized that it was true. *The first opera gloves I'd ever seen,* his mother had told him, *and hair like tinsel.* That night he went home and scrutinized every Busby Berkeley still he had, the complicated layouts of legs and smiles, looking to find his aunt.

It became his hobby—"My quest," he told friends. For years he went to MGM features at the revival houses, watched television specials about the early days in Hollywood, bought splashy picturebooks about Busby Berkeley. But he had no idea what to look for: his own aunt, on those sound stages that looked big as the Grand Canyon? It was unimaginable, like angels or particle physics. When the camera zoomed past the line Paul could only see what everyone saw—identical legs, fans, smiles.

Now that he was thirty-four, he lived a life without excesses. His love for the old style was as fierce as ever, but he understood that he was in a world of gasoline conservation and escalating crime rates. He only went to the old movies when his girlfriend Gloria wanted to go. They saw the same people at those movies—*Follies, Golddiggers of 1933*—again and again. The women crimped marcel waves into their hair, the men wore white dinner jackets and carried cigarettes in silver cases. They made Paul uncomfortable, coming to the movies dressed in boas and silk shoes from boutiques along Melrose Avenue. It was one thing to admire style, to have an eye for line. But this was something else. Did he have to *tell* them it wasn't 1933 anymore?

Gloria had her own supply of boas and bias-cut evening gowns, and Paul knew she had stopped wearing them because of him. He was grateful, and it was perhaps in return that he told her, the night after his mother called, about Frances. He regretted it instantly, as her eyes caught fire. "She must have wonderful stories to tell," Gloria said. "You could write a book."

"It isn't as if we were close. I never met her."

"Still," Gloria said. "What glamour." Paul knew she was imagining, remembering Gloria Swanson in *Sunset Boulevard.*

"That's me," he said. "Glamour glamour glamour." Until his mother's phone call, he hadn't thought of Frances for ten years. His time was filled with the magazine, its demands, the minutia of alignment and balance. How long had it been since he had been captivated by the old world, his blood beating in his temples and throat until it threatened to bear him away? When Gloria said he should go to visit her in the home and ask her a few questions about the movies before it was too late, he shrugged and said why not.

No matter where she is, Stella sits quietly. She has moved enough. People have learned to leave her alone; she will not play games or watch television, she will not eat birthday cake, even her own. She has a trim waist still, if anyone cares to look.

What Stella chooses to do every day is stare. After dressing in the morning—the only movement she willingly makes—she looks at blank surfaces: her closet door, the windowsill in the main room, the soft adobe wall of the courtyard below. Stella's eyesight is strong, she has the best vision in the home; she knows what she's looking at. She seeks out these flat expanses that are uninterrupted by color or dimension.

Very few people have heard her speak. Her voice is fine, husky and vibrant, but talking, like moving, is something she chooses not to do. She appears content, she is as mild as ice, she is left alone.

She has learned that by sitting with her limbs locked the voice she hears fades. Whenever she moves it begins to talk to her again, as if encouraged. It is up to her to keep the proper distance between them. She presses her lips to keep from answering, and when her arms yearn to lift up in response, she tells herself they are encased in rock, thick and heavy as buildings. She plummets into sleep at night, weary from having carried such weight on her frail bones.

Paul arrived with a mixed bouquet. It struck him as a charming gesture when he saw the Chicano boy at the light at Fairfax and Santa Monica Boulevard, and Paul gave him two dollars for the small bouquet, daisies and baby's breath and a single rose. He planned to give the flowers to Frances with a bow.

When he walked into the home—the entrance gave way to a large room—the dozen inhabitants swiveled toward him. If there had been conversation, it was silenced. Paul hadn't expected an audience, and with nothing prepared to say to these watchful old people, he looked down at the bouquet. He was gripping the stems so tightly he could feel moisture seeping between his fingers. *I should have gotten a big one,* he thought.

None of the people looking at him resembled his idea of Frances, but how could he be sure? So many years, and all he could guess was a 1920s siren—plump, inviting. He could feel a tiny smile quaking at the corners of his mouth. "Frances Murphy?" A woman near him shook her head. He couldn't control his expression, could neither smile nor not smile, and he could feel his mouth fluttering under his moustache. "My aunt? Frances? I'm here to visit?"

He knew what they were thinking. Anyone could see, in the glare of their eyes. Spotlighted so suddenly, he felt guilty and muddled as a movie gangster. So many years, no effort, not a card. He knew they would tell him he had no claim to her. But they were wrong. If he had to, if they forced him, he'd tell them everything; how she'd always been important to him, even before he knew about her, even during the quiet years. What they were seeing was not neglect. Why, she was part of him—she was who he *was.* How many movies had he seen, looking for her? To this day he bought books of '30s stills. If he found her he would frame the picture, mount it on his wall, tell visitors about his aunt who had been in the movies. *You see?* he was ready to say. *How wrong you are. I've never forgotten about her. Not once.*

"Flowers. How thoughtful. Who are you here to see?"

The nurse, face as smooth and bland as an egg, had arrived silently behind him. "Frances," he muttered. "Frances Murphy."

The nurse's eyebrows went up. She looked, Paul thought, like a kewpie doll. "Well! Won't she be surprised. Do you know where her room is?"

"No. I've never been here before."

The nurse indicated a corridor to his left. "If you leave your flowers at the nurses' station, they'll find you a vase." Paul nodded—he had no intention of giving them up now—and set off down the hallway, the stems stuck to his fingers.

But when he came to her door he hesitated. Would she be asleep? Dressed? None of the other doors were closed. He could still go home now. He could leave the flowers with the nurses, leave a card with them, promise to be back tomorrow, next week, often. Maybe there was a back door he could slip through. He glanced behind him and saw how the corridor simply ended, cut off abruptly as a stump. The nurse who had sent him here was probably still in the big room, waiting with the residents for his return.

Paul knocked gingerly on Frances's door. The hallway was quiet, and he felt large and conspicuous. Faced with the blank door, holding flowers, he could have been a rejected beau. What was he waiting for? His mother had told him that even twenty-five years earlier Frances wouldn't answer a door. He put his hand on her doorknob and plunged into the room, brandishing her flowers before him.

When Stella has bad nights, she hears the voice for days afterwards. Even if she lies still as stone she hears it, hot and liquid and intimate. *When you came back you had leaves in your hair. I made you keep them there, so people could see you'd been rolling. We did the screen test with your hair full of leaves.* Stella awakened this morning panting, her shoulders aching as if she had pushed a great weight all night. There were long scratches on her legs, so she dressed herself early, before anyone could see and force her to be examined. She cannot abide being touched.

I picked you out first. Legs, hair. You figured out just what I wanted. Never had to direct you. If she looks at anything that moves, if she looks at bright colors or patterns, they remind her. She has followed all the patterns and worn every color. She was told how to trace shapes until she saw how her legs would open and reach to make stars, roses, whatever was wanted. It was her body that was used to describe costumes to the wardrobe mistress, Stella's body to show how the waist should come, and the bust. *I made her cut everything high on the leg because of you. I made you wear short jackets and robes. The day the leaves were in your hair you came wearing a man's shirt and high heels and never said a word.*

Stella understands what she must do. She dresses in soft slacks and sweaters—she is often cold—and finds plain things to look at. She has discovered hairline cracks in the plaster, paint bubbles, faint chalk marks on the adobe wall. Sometimes even these are too much, and she looks at blank paper or the white sheets on her bed. She is weepy and exhausted by the time she finally hears only her own silence, and she will distrust sleep for weeks, because of what it has brought her.

Gloria was waiting at Paul's apartment when he got home. She wanted to hear all about it.

"You want to know the truth? It wasn't much." Paul was talking from the kitchen, where he poured himself a glass of wine. Gloria stayed on the couch and called her questions back to him.

"How did she look? Is she still beautiful?"

"Frances? Glo, she was a chorus girl, not Lillian Gish."

"Well, glamourous then. Does she still look like Hollywood?"

"No." Paul stood at the edge of the living room holding a water glass full of chablis. "She looks like a mouse. She's tiny and curled up."

"Remember how Rita Hayworth looked at the end?" Gloria asked. "Nobody could believe it. Fat, hair all matted."

"She's very tidy." She looked, although he didn't tell Gloria this, as though she'd licked herself clean, like a small, fastidious animal.

"So was she happy to see you? She must have been surprised."

"I don't think she knew who I was." She hadn't looked happy or surprised. She hadn't looked at him at all.

"Well," Gloria said swiftly. "We can hardly expect her to remember too well anymore." She paused, watching him in the doorway. "What did she have to say? What did she tell you?"

"Nothing." Paul drank off a finger of the wine. "She didn't tell
me anything." He'd stood before her, large and foolish, attempting
light conversation while she stared at the wall behind his elbow. He
kept explaining who he was, telling her his name again and again.
He told her how devoted he was to the old movies, her career, and
how he would love to hear stories of those days. How he'd always
wished he could have been a part of that wonderful elegance, how
he felt her past connected them in a powerful way. Finally, how
guilty he felt for not having written, done anything, kept her from
this place. How things had come in the way, but that he'd never
stopped thinking about her, looking for her. He'd blundered out of
her room like a bear, leaving the flowers scattered over the thin
bedspread.

"Aren't you glad you went to see her?" Gloria asked.

"Oh yes. Glad."

"I'm sure she's pleased that you came."

"No question about it. Her face lit right up."

"At least you tried," she said. "She might have been full of
memories. You couldn't have known without trying."

"And now I know," said Paul.

He went to bed early that night and slept poorly. At work he was
groggy and had trouble concentrating—twice the intern who was
working with them for a semester had to point out lines of type that
sloped clumsily up the boards. Paul kept rearranging the heads to
make them balance, but all he could see was the pattern the words
made tumbling across the page. He stayed in the office until ten
o'clock that night, trying fruitlessly to make sense of the letters
under his fingers.

Another new orderly has come; it happens here often. They are
young, their hands not gentle. This one wheeled her to the lunchroom at noon, leaving her nothing to look at. She eats a little, so no
one will attempt to feed her, then searches for some blank surface.

Even her napkin has a fine, busy pattern pressed on it, white-on-white lines coming together before her eyes to make diamonds and stars.

I'll do one someday that makes your body. I'll make you to music, and all the cameras going. The floor too, the linoleum that runs through the home, has lines and splashes as precise as Morse code. On the yellow walls are sayings, small posters, a group of drawings from a local grade school. The ceiling tiles are patterned with small holes. *You came to me with leaves in your hair. All you have to do is know what to look for. You knew how to make a man.*

She concentrates on sitting motionless in the wheelchair. Eventually the voice will rise up and wash over her, and then she will be simple again. All she has to do is refuse to respond. It is more difficult than anyone could ever imagine.

Later, an orderly recognizes the mistake and takes her back to her room. Looking at the light bedspread, Stella can see the greenish stain left by the stems of flowers.

Paul's visit to his aunt ruptured his life in ways he hadn't expected. When the intern neglected to bring Paul's mail to his office one morning, Paul screamed at him, saying, "You had so many better things to do, you couldn't bring a handful of letters ten feet? Just too *wrapped up?*" He set to opening the mail with such force that he ripped one of the flats clear across and had to have the photo reshot.

Nothing was satisfying him. His apartment was too dark, the drapes that he had spent hours pleating and hanging looked awkward and stagey. He gathered them up to rearrange and choked on the dust that flew from fabric gone so long untouched.

It was as if everything was suddenly dim and blurred at the edges—even Gloria looked faded, her clothing bunched, her gestures affected and pathetic. When Paul decided to go again to see Frances, he knew enough not to tell Gloria.

He could not have said why he was going—he successfully talked himself out of the return visit three times before he slammed out of the office and pointed the car east. He didn't bring family photo albums. He didn't take advantage of the time on the freeway to frame questions or small talk. He didn't, of course, bring flowers, and so felt less awkward when he opened the door to her room to find her just as he'd left her two weeks before.

"I wanted to see you again," he said. "I haven't been able to sleep since I saw you."

What had he expected? That she would rise up to embrace him once he stopped compulsively introducing himself? She sat dully across from him, old, old, and he could feel her suffering him in the block of sunlight opposite her chair.

"I want to know what happened to you," he said. She was tiny— probably smaller now than when she had been dancing for Busby Berkeley. He studied her face, superimposing the smooth, round cheeks, the guileless eyes. Glancing at her legs, he imagined her throwing aside the lap robe and chair. Imagined the proud, wide fan-kicks of *Stairway to Paradise.*

He crossed the room, stood by the window, and looked out into the ugly courtyard with its thick wall. "Why did you stop? Didn't you want to go on, be a star?" He was, he realized, furious. She could have gone on. She could have done Ruby Keeler better—she could have blazed everyone else off the screen. Her own self, brighter than all the rest—it would have been her legacy.

"You were Hollywood!" he said. "When that meant something. The whole world watching. I'd give my right arm—leg, too—to know that anybody was watching me." He turned back to her and he could feel how his voice was becoming wheedling, reedy and desperate the way it had sounded when he was seventeen and violent to touch a girl. "There's no one else in the family who even came close. You should have. You didn't know what it meant. You owed it to me."

In his rush out of the room Paul nearly collided with the nurse, who drew back and smiled at him. "I'm sure Frances appreciated your visit," she said.

"Why doesn't she talk?"

"She's capable. She speaks when she has things she cares to say. She's very well-mannered. Quite a lady."

"She sits and stares."

"Well, she is getting on. You can't be expecting too much of her. She dresses herself every morning. We're quite proud."

"She used to—" there it was again, the reediness, the harshness back in his throat "—be in the movies. Did you know that?"

"Well, isn't that interesting."

"She should be talking."

"I'm sure she'll speak up whenever anything is on her mind."

"Why don't you spend time with her, ask her things?"

She smiled, and Paul wanted to slap her. "This is a facility for many people, all of whom need our help. If you would like extra attention for your relative, then I encourage you to give her the kind of time you feel she needs."

She danced for Busby Berkeley. Thousands of people saw her. "I'll look into it," he muttered. *Get her the hell away from you. Let her stay with people who know what it means to do what she did.* Driving home he went far out of his way, sweeping into the valley and then up the dusty lanes until he rose high enough to see the ocean over the hills, vague and hazy blue, a backdrop for any action a man might choose to take.

Stella's own voice wakes her. She doesn't know how loudly she cried out—they only come for screams that are high and hard, not for the ordinary night murmurs of the aged—and so she lies still, listening for footsteps. She studies the top of her sheet, still smooth from her motionless sleep. If they come they will ask her what she was dreaming, and she will not know. Already, she does not know.

She is nearly ready to give up. She knows that her age is playing tricks on her, but she is longing to move again, to dance. She almost believes that the only thing holding her back is her own will. If she imagines making even the simplest gesture her mind magnifies it into something grand and beautiful—bending to pick up a thread would become a sweeping curtsey; in raising her hand to smooth her hair she will acknowledge all the world. There is no middle ground: If she reaches toward the attendant it will be her undoing. It is this that is so enticing.

The voice has become constant, companionable. She is beginning to think it will never stop again. It chats while she sits or eats, it accompanies her as she wheels from room to room. It brings up everything: running, stumbling, laughing with the other girls on the sand at Santa Monica; falling—eight, ten of them sometimes—into a rumble seat and driving into the hills, hilarious with illegal champagne. Stella is astonished at the exactitude of the voice's memories.

There are the other memories as well, when the voice begins to murmur and darken. *Opening. Like the center of a flower. Like fire.*

They'd all known what he was doing, it was hardly any secret as he called the complex directions from his high director's chair behind the lights. They pointed and flexed and wheeled for him in patterns only he could see. Of course they'd known. They'd envied her, wearing his shirt, the leaves he put in her hair. But when he stopped, and the new girl appeared next to her—next to her!—in the line, what was left to do with that knowledge, that opening flame? Having a talent only for arranging her legs as directed, what was she to do with a body that throbbed and rose?

"I can't hold it—it's too hard," she screams.

A few minutes later, when the attendants arrive, she turns to them confidentially. "He never should have taught me that. Did he think I was going to forget? I've never been so ashamed." She has never since known those things—passion. Glory.

Paul admitted his obsession after his second visit. He was dreaming about her tiny, precise body and half-wild eyes. He knew better than to tell anyone—dear God, she was eighty-four—but her image was always there, shadowy behind the magazine layouts, the traffic on the San Diego freeway, Gloria's face.

"*Lullabye of Broadway* tonight at the Los Feliz," she said over the phone. "I can meet you at the office."

"Can't. Bluelines look terrible—I'll be here all night. I'll call you later this week."

"Tonight's the last night. After that it's something Italian."

"Nothing I can do. Blues look like they were set with a rubber ruler." He was telling the truth—the pages of the central spread looked terrible. The intern must have thought they were supposed to look misaligned and clumsy. "Better go without me."

"No fun to go alone. You can't get the kid to fix them?"

"Glo, every once in a while they like me to pay attention to my job. It's a little masquerade we put on around here."

He would call her later, when he felt contrite. The headline on the board staggered across two pages, and he bent to measure it against the block of type under his hands. She had no sense of his life, the sharp and particular satisfaction of aligning shape and line and image. She'd never understood for even a moment. How attentive he had to be for form revealing itself; a change in column width, in font, in color or shape or format would alter everything.

It was still in the office. The advertising department had raucously left at six, and he heard nothing from editorial. There was the luxury of quiet time around him like water, and Paul began to relax. Perhaps he would, after all, take the entire night with his precise squares and rulers, the color wheel. This was the part of his job he had always enjoyed the most—more, even, than the shoots with famous people, stars. When his hands were on the type he understood everything he needed to do. So after finishing the center layout he set to work on the rest of the magazine.

He made adjustments of a hair's breadth in spacing and alignment. He could feel the magazine coming together for him, as complete and ornamental as a rose. His hands were light and elastic; he was content. More than content, he was exhilarated. As long as the images were shifting before him, it didn't matter that people—the public—would see the magazine without ever once imagining him, what he did.

At two A.M. the work suddenly dropped away and there was nothing else he could do. He left the pages to be re-shot and drove restlessly into the heavy night. He couldn't stop trying to see with order and definition, and he looked at the billboards on Sunset Boulevard and the heavy traffic through Hollywood as if he could rearrange them, establish balance and beauty. He wasn't satisfied until he drove high into the hills, where he could see the headlights from three freeways swirl and mesh. He sat under eucalyptus trees, the dusty and aromatic leaves crumbling down his back and in his hair. A person could only understand from a distance, he thought. It didn't have to do with individual components—words, images—it wasn't that at all. The importance was in thousands of interchangeable parts, tiny as stars. The constant pulse of cars approaching and receding—who knew if they were the same cars racing again and again across the interchanges? It made no difference. The patterns were etched into the orange Los Angeles night. He had never seen anything so beautiful.

Showered and freshly shaved, he was at the door of the home the next morning at nine. *Did you understand how necessary you were? Did you understand how you could be replaced?* he was going to ask. The milk-faced nurse met him to say that Frances was in restraints. There had been screams.

"She spent a difficult night," she said.

"I need to talk to her," Paul said.

"I can't imagine that will make any difference."

"This is important."

She shrugged. "I don't know what you expect to get out of it."

"That's my business." She lifted her eyebrows and then stepped back from the door, allowing him in. Paul was four steps toward Frances's room before he turned back to the nurse. "You don't know the first thing about her," he said. "I know what she needs. I love her." He turned back down the hallway then, the nurse's stunned face his first augury of triumph.

Stella has been waiting, so it is no surprise to her when the voice comes again. Unable as she is to move or succumb to any temptations, she is relaxed. This is what she has been waiting for, the voice washing over and around her. Submerged, she cannot be expected to respond. *Everything comes together. You knew that right from the beginning, didn't you?* She doesn't know what she knew from the beginning. She has always carried more knowledge than she wanted. This is what men have given her.

She is not unaware that there is a man standing next to her bed. She imagines that if she could stretch out she could touch him. She imagines she knows what he would feel like. This is not important. She pays attention only to the rise and fall of the voice washing around her, over her head. Perhaps it will carry her away.

The leaves, the way it smelled. It all came together. It was impossible without you. Stella smiles. She feels utterly weightless, and realizes that she is being held down because without the restraints she would float straight to the ceiling. *You showed me everything.*

You made me She imagines bobbing at the ceiling, her nose bumping against the tiles. *It should never have taken me so long.*

"No," she says, and the voice stops. She is back on her bed again, the thick, frayed cuffs clenching her wrists.

"What? No, what?" It is the man beside the bed talking, a man's voice beside her bed. It is the one she could perhaps touch, were she free of this rough canvas.

"So long. Long." She's beginning to forget. Words have always slipped away from her. *You came and didn't say a word.* It's movement, gestures repeated, that she can trust.

The voice in her room is talking. It is talking about patterns; it has always talked about patterns. She pays it no attention—she would like to float again. It has been years since she has felt so simple, as if she were dwelling at the exact center of her life. She closes her eyes and sees lines making perfect patterns. These please her. *After you I saw things better. Until you, I didn't know how a body could* She is seeing patterns opening out, taking her in. When she opens her eyes she sees the man opening his hands toward her.

"Yes," she says.

Paul, frightened, triumphant, half delirious with the blood drumming through him, leaned to the straps. He could scarcely control his fingers—the simple buckle seemed beyond him—but he was wild to take her away, and she passive beneath him and smiling. When the last of the straps fell he bent to slip his arms under her back and legs, then staggered under her weight. Who could have imagined her solidity, this real body? *Real, real.*

She was as pliant as a girl, and he was roaring. The need to make her tell him, teach him all the things she knew. He felt how she formed around his arms, how she curled there, even as his shoulders quivered with the weight, slight as it was, of her body.

He couldn't move. His arms began to drop in tortured increments and he knew he must hurry, knew he must hasten to the light and brilliance outside this tight, boxed-in place, but his knees were locked and his feet immobile on the linoleum floor. He gazed at Frances as if at a picture, seeing the exquisite webbing around her eyes and mouth, the smallness of her hands. He stared and stared.

Her eyes were bright as water. His arms had dropped to waist level when Frances began gently to kick. First one foot, then the other, her toes pointed inside her soft slippers. She moved her legs through the air gracefully. Paul's arms shook as if palsied, but he clutched at her with reserves of endurance he couldn't have guessed at and watched as she kicked, gaining strength and elevation, the slender old legs pointing up over the arm that held them. They were gracious gestures. He had never seen anything so beautiful.

Her legs cut through and molded the air. Paul watched against the drumming in his ears, the convulsive throbbing of his arms, saw the air itself take shape. He knew he could not continue to hold her. Who could have guessed she would take such strength to sustain? But for as long as he could he watched her legs beat out their perfect time, as if they were showing him secrets. As if they were giving him everything he had ever wanted to have.

Until It Comes Closer

Sometimes I still wait for my sister to come back. Days I get up and expect any minute to see her. I'll find myself watching the road, staring behind the baking soda or up over the closet door. I have dreams that she comes home all alone, the two of us looking at each other in a morning cool and still.

For a while, other people came. Neighbors dropped by at all hours with casseroles, then sniffed around the house in case I had her hidden behind the curtains. People who'd never in their lives done more than nod in the church service showed up with covered dishes at seven o'clock in the morning. They said ugly things, quoted Scripture on shouldering burdens as if they had the faintest idea what they were talking about. Then finally they got bored having only me to look at, nothing out of the ordinary. "Don't you miss her?" Mardis George asked me once, and I wanted to say, What do you think? She was my *sister*. But we make decisions, and we steer by whatever lights we see.

Mostly, I've gotten used to living on my own. It's quiet, and there are things to tend to—I raked all the gutters, and set out twenty-five tomato seedlings. Time soon for squash and eggplant, all the summer's busyness. Now it's warm, I've been keeping the shades up in all the rooms, the windows wide, and I can see out in every direction. The vines outside reach right into the rooms.

It's just sometimes that I wake up sudden, as if I heard Martha. Or someone will say something, like Louise at the market wondering how I could bear to let her go, she was such a sweet thing. As if she was my pet. What's worse is when the dreams come, and I see myself standing in a field, Martha being carried away from me in a high wind. I can't do a thing to save her.

I can see now how my mama knew this would happen. When she was alive she never took Martha out, never introduced her to anybody, hardly let her know she lived in the world. Everything Martha knew was what she saw on TV. I only wish Mama had explained herself to me. Because I saw how she'd pack Martha down in her chair when she was getting ready to leave, or pick Martha up and put her in her room when folks came, and I thought she was ashamed. I'd march into Martha's room and play with her until people were gone, even though she wasn't much fun to play with—what could she do? she hardly knew anything—and then come out after to glare at my mama.

Martha was five years old before she saw a feather firsthand— that's how long it was before anyone thought to bring her one. It was a pitiful thing. She was right there in the middle of our lives—from the time she was born we could never all go out together, somebody had to tend her—but all we did was feed her and make sure she was warm. Daddy couldn't stand to be in the same room with her. He'd look at her, his mouth going soft, and he'd start to rock himself and moan in a hushy voice until my mama would hurry in and take him away. And there would be Martha, her eyes big, wondering what she'd done.

He passed on when Martha was eight; I was thirteen. I came home and told her all about the funeral, the flag and the guns, how Mama had looked tall and beautiful. There'd been a man there in a wheelchair, and I told her about him, too, how everyone had cleared a respectful space at the side of the grave. Martha looked up sharp at that and I told her his pant legs were full and soft, like they'd been stuffed with cotton rags. She dropped her eyes again and made me nervous, so I kept telling about the funeral, remembering everything for her, but she didn't look up anymore.

It was after the funeral that my mama had people come to look at Martha, who was scared frozen. She'd never had to talk to anyone but us and the doctor, had hardly even seen anyone else—the milkman, the mailman, people on TV. Then all of a sudden Mama was propping her up in the living room and men in uniforms filed through to look. One of them actually picked her up and turned her around like she was a paperweight until she began to bellow and Mama snatched her back again. Mama began to stay up late every night with a typewriter, tapping out page after page, and Martha got so she shook all the time, even when I was just telling her about school like I'd done every day for years.

It wasn't like it was a secret—Mama told me right out. "I think Martha was hurt because of something they gave your daddy when he was fighting," she told me. "I'm trying to do something about it. I'm trying to get some justice for your sister." It didn't matter to me. It wasn't going to get arms and legs for her, so I didn't see the use. I spent a lot of time outside playing. I can remember those days clear as clear, they seemed to go on forever: Mama typing through the nights, the men coming and asking questions—"Do you get fevers? Do you get blisters under your tongue?"—Martha shaking like a chill at anything, even her own sister coming through the door.

Then it was over. We'd been getting letters from Washington so steady that I didn't pay them attention—the eagle envelopes came as often as fliers from the IGA. But when the last one got there my mama knew it was different right off; she grabbed it out of my hands and opened it in front of the mailbox where anybody could see her. She didn't move while she read it, but her mouth got hard as wood. When she finally turned around and stomped back into the house, I stayed with her close.

She got into the kitchen and stopped to read the letter again, then folded it perfectly along the creases and put it back in the envelope she'd half shredded. She was standing with her back to me but she knew I was there. "Go somewhere else," she said. I didn't move. She reached into the high cupboard above the stove and pulled down a bottle. "I'm warning you," she said, still not looking at me, "you'd better make yourself scarce or you'll wish you had."

"Where'm I gonna go?" I asked her, cocksure and dumb like kids are.

She turned around so quick her sleeves puffed up with the breeze. "You better *find* yourself a place, sister, and you might as well start finding it right now. You just find yourself a hole and lay right down in it. You'll need it, and I can promise you there's nobody else will do it for you.''

It was five years before she died, but within a year she'd drunk herself down to a kernel. Nights, I'd come home and spoon the same food into three mouths—first Martha's, then Mama's, then I'd make myself eat some too. We managed until Martha got an infection, her fever up so high I could see the blood racing under that silk-white skin. When the doctor came he wrote out a prescription and handed it to me.

"My mama—" I started to say.

"Can't do a thing for herself," he cut in. "You hurry now to get this filled. I'll wait with your sister until you get back." Mama stayed slumped in the corner of the sofa, and when I got to the drugstore, Bert filled the prescription without any questions.

Martha and I survived, we lived day after day. What else was there to do? I put one foot in front of the other. I tried bringing her things from outside to look at—little things, leaves and stones—but after a while I quit. What good was it for her to have a stone, if she'd never felt the water in a creek? But I told her everything I knew about people and things, so she'd know more than what she saw on TV. She got to where she asked questions, even though she hushed whenever anyone was there. People thought she was retarded on top of everything else, but she was just shy. Smart too, as it turned out—smarter than me, because when I first came up with the idea of taking her out, she said no. She said it would change everything, and she didn't want people looking at her. How did she know? I thought it was just what she needed, and said so.

"We'll just go by ourselves, take back roads. A wheelchair doesn't make much noise. Nobody'll mind us. You're a part of this world, Martha, and it's not fair that you don't know anything about it.'' Well, I was right too, and anybody could see it. Once I had the idea it was with me all the time, bright as morning, and even though Martha kept telling me that it wasn't smart and it wouldn't work, she knew my mind was made up. Eventually she asked me to leave the little window in her room open so she could get used to the cool air on her face, and I knew she was done fighting.

I started to get us ready. I outfitted Martha's wheelchair with wide tires like a bike's, and I practiced pushing it up the valley behind the house, loading it down with encyclopedias that weighed more than Martha did. I fixed her some new clothes, the first she'd had in Lord knows how long, and I bought us both ponchos. I put together a lightweight kit for food that we'd buy on the road, and fixed a basket on the back of the chair for the flashlight, tent, matches, and all Martha's supplies—we were *ready* for things. I got myself sturdy boots. The day before we left I went to the bank and took out seven hundred and fifty dollars. Lucille looked surprised when I told her how much I wanted and she handed the money to me slow, giving me plenty of time to explain. I put it in my purse and walked out. What business was it of hers?

In the morning I sat with Martha and spread the section map of Indiana in front of her. It was our second map; we'd gone over the first one so many times, tracing routes and then changing our minds and trying to erase, that it had disintegrated. Martha didn't have the faintest idea how the maps connected with roads or things to see, but she could follow the spidery lines better with her eyes than I could using my finger, so I made her navigator. I pinned the map down over her so she could see how we followed the blue lines that branched up the page. I put sweaters on both of us and locked the door as we went out.

It was a pretty morning, the kind that feels clean. Looking down at Martha, I could see how tense she was—she was pushing herself back against the chair, and her eyes were big and wild. She had gone out a time or two into the backyard, but in ten steps we'd be on land she'd never seen in all her life. "Where to, navigator?" I asked her. It wouldn't have done any good to slow down then.

"North," she muttered, and I knew she didn't have any idea which of those valley walls was north. She wasn't even looking ahead, just staring at the tree branches locked together over our heads. I started pushing up the hill to the north road as fast as I could. After the encyclopedias, Martha's weight was nothing at all, no more than a handful of feathers.

These were the hills and woods I'd run around since I was a girl. These were trees I'd climbed and hid in, and secret places where I used to flush out rabbits, and I kept pointing all of them out to

Martha as we rolled by. Places I'd been running and jumping in since I was half her age, less. There were no people nearby, and the crunch of the heavy wheels on leaves and twigs was scaring away birds and animals. It was probably just as well. In that mild morning, light coming down easy on our heads, Martha was squeezed back tight in her chair, and if she could have managed to say anything I know she would have told me to turn around, right there on the spot. I talked a blue streak, I've never found myself with so much to say. If we went back then, before we even left our own land, she'd never go out again. She never would see anything simple and skittish as a squirrel firsthand, and maybe it was selfish of me, but I couldn't stand that.

Just as Martha was starting to rediscover her voice and little whimpers were bubbling out, we cleared the top of the ridge and bumped onto the hard dirt road. "This is the way I used to walk to school," I told her, and slowed down. "The older kids used to stand right off to the edge here and wait to scare the little ones on their way home."

"Did they?" she asked. "Scare you?"

"They never did. I knew they were there." I waited for Martha to say something else, but she stayed quiet. When I looked down at her I thought maybe she was just a hair less tense—at least she didn't seem to be backed up so hard against the chair. I slowed way down, so the sound of the wheels and the creak of the chair softened, and I put my hand on top of Martha's head. I was going to say something, find some words to reassure her, I don't know what, but a mockingbird dropped like a rock from a tree a few feet ahead of us and Martha was plastered to the back of the chair again, even after it swooped back up and started singing in that mean way they have.

"A mockingbird. That's all. We'll see them all over," I said. I felt helpless. For weeks I'd been telling her how, if she stayed still, animals might come. I'd been telling her how pure it feels to have a chipmunk come up close, or a squirrel. Now here she was terrified of a mockingbird. "Martha—"

"I thought it was going to fall," she interrupted me. "It came down so fast, and I didn't see where it was coming from, and I didn't know it meant to do that."

"They're like that," I said. "Pretty, isn't it?"

"I can't tell. I can't see it, way up there. I'll have to wait until it comes closer."

I wasn't about to tell her then about mockingbirds, how we could stay there all week and wouldn't see any more of that bird. Sweat was running down her neck and mine—it was a good enough time to rest. We stayed in the shady part of the road and the bird kept singing away. I don't know how long we were there. I was uncomfortable, but I couldn't shift my weight because the bird would hear me and that would be the end of it. For once I knew enough to keep quiet, and I watched the air dry the sweat on Martha's neck. I thought my patience had given out half a hundred times before that bird flew down to a lower branch, where we could almost see him. The sun hit the feathers on his tail, we could see them shine. I knew it was the best we were going to do, that bright purple and black, but Martha was staring and quiet as a wall, so I stayed quiet too.

Then the bird jumped right down onto the dirt in front of Martha's chair and pecked around for something to eat. We could see his big cocky head and how the white band on his wing folded into his body. I'd never been so close to a bird—for a second I forgot about Martha and craned to see better. The bird marched around in front of us so I could see the hard scales on its skinny legs and how its beak was dull yellow. "Just look at that thing!" I couldn't help whispering. It flew off then, straight up as if pulled by a string. And Martha said, "I always thought it would look like that."

After that, everything got easy. She asked me to pin her hair up so she could feel the breeze on her neck. We stopped to have lunch and by nightfall we'd pushed maybe five miles. There were trees I wasn't sure I'd seen before, and I couldn't tell her who lived in the houses and farms we passed. "Tomorrow," I said as I pitched our tent off under some oaks, "it'll be as new to me as to you."

"That'll be good," she said.

We'd only seen one person all day, and that was across a wide field. He'd waved to us, and I stopped to wave back, swinging my arm across the air as if he was the person we'd hoped, all along, we'd see.

For one week it was perfect. In the mornings I'd get up first and find a store—I had to get Martha milk every day—and then I'd get

Martha up, put her hair up and sunblock on, make us breakfast. She didn't fuss like she did at home. Most of the time she didn't say anything at all. I'd be talking about the walk over, the folks at the store, the funny little towns we were skirting, and I'd look to see her staring at grass, or the moss on a rock. "What is that?" she'd ask.

"It's just moss. You've seen moss before." She'd glance at me and turn back to the moss, and I'd feel ridiculous. Who puts pictures of moss on TV?

We made about ten miles a day. We weren't in any hurry. We were touring, after all, no timetable, and pushing Martha up some of those soft-looking hills slowed our pace. I opened my eyes wide for new things to show her and I started seeing animals I'd never been able to find on my own—muskrats, foxes. "Look at the skinny little fingers on that thing," I whispered at Martha when we saw the raccoon. "Look like they could pick a lock."

"I saw one yesterday when you were off at the store," Martha said. "I saw it wash its hands."

"Well, shoot. You might have told a person. You seeing elephants too?"

"Don't think so," she said without looking away from the raccoon. "Saw a porcupine, though."

"Maybe you should start pointing out the things you see with those X-ray eyes."

"They don't come around so much when you're here. You make too much noise."

By the end of the week we were pushing out of the hills into the central flat of the state. Martha kept guiding us straight north, I don't know why. We could feel the air begin to change; the sweet breeze quit and the only birds we heard were far away. Hot, damp air settled on our faces and shoulders like wet flannel. "You sure you want to go this way?" I kept asking. "We don't need to keep going the same way. We can go east, too. Over to the river."

"I like this," she'd say. "I want to see all kinds of country, not just what you want to see."

But there was less to see all the time. As the ground leveled around us, the trees gave out and we found ourselves looking across broad fields, the corn barely as high as my knees. You could see a person standing two acres away plain as day. Martha and I couldn't have stuck out more if we'd been billboards. The farmers and their wives standing at the edge of their land could watch our steady progress all afternoon.

"If we went off to the east it would be prettier," I told her. "We could go down to the Ohio River. You've never seen a big river."

"I've never seen corn," she said. "Never even seen one of these farm houses, the way you keep backing away from them."

I'd been thinking she wouldn't notice. I didn't see any point in going right up to people; we didn't leave home to look at people. I'd just wanted to make sure she saw *things,* the rocks and grass and plain air that everybody else has without even thinking about. I thought that much was her due. She could look at animals, and they wouldn't stare back at her. You could trust them for common decency. But we'd left the animals behind us in all the thickets and bushes, and ever since we'd come down into this wide-open land I'd had the feeling we were being watched by bright, greedy eyes. As it was, we'd already been stopped once, when a car pulled over and a lady with hair piled like a Church of Christer got out. "Can I *help?*" she asked, her eyes on Martha like they were nailed there.

"No ma'am, we're fine, just out walking," I told her. "My sister and I just taking the air." And Martha not saying a word.

"Well isn't that—*fine.* Why, you must devote your whole life to her, poor thing." She stared and stared, like she was memorizing.

"We work together," I said, ugly, and fresh as cheese. Mama'd always told me that vinegar won't catch flies, and I was trying to get this woman with her hair and her flowered dress to *leave.*

"Why what could she—" But I was already pushing, shooting down the road so fast I could have made sparks, telling Martha that there are fools everywhere, to pay her no heed. Martha didn't answer, and looking down, I couldn't read her face.

We couldn't find nice places to sleep anymore. The air at night was sticky and heavy in our throats, and there weren't any more closed-in groves. I'd walk a half-mile off the road and just put up the tent, as big and plain as a thumb sticking up out of the ground. I'd waken five times in the night and there would be no noise around us. I kept thinking that it must have been a person out there. We'd hear *something,* the trilling of birds when the sun came up, if we were by ourselves. But even Martha couldn't bring birds near us now. And she acted like she didn't see any changes, like everything was the same. As long as we were alone, she talked a blue streak.

"That's some corn," she liked to say, jutting out her chin. "Heat keep up like this, it'll be harvest in July."

"You don't know what you're talking about."

"Might could be a farmer. Got a feel for these things." She banged against the back of the chair, happy as a pig in rain.

"You can't wheel a chair between those rows. Where you going to get a foreman?"

"At the getting place." She banged back again, grinning herself silly.

So we kept going. Even in the morning the sky was the color of cement, and Martha's fine hair stuck to my fingers when I tried to braid it. We plodded through the landscape, me wiping the sweat out of our eyes. I don't know why I kept on. I could have turned around anytime, could have said we were out of money, it was time to go back. But Martha was hell-bent to go north, as if something was waiting for her there, and it got so I forgot I could do anything except what she wanted. She said things, I couldn't even imagine where she got them. Squinting at the sunset, she muttered, "Sailor's delight." Or just looking ahead, down the gravel access road, "Tinker's damn." As if she were testing out the words, running her thumb along them to check for sharpness. And I was steady and dumb as a mule, pushing her one step after another, not even seeing anymore where we were going.

It was a night we were just outside of Eminence that I started to look around again, and by then it was too late. We were in the tent early because it had gotten too hot to push anymore, and there was no place for us to wait out the sun, there in the open. So we lay quiet, the late-day light pricking in through all the tiny holes in the canvas. Martha was having trouble breathing, and her skin had gone the chalky color of old milk.

"I think it might be time to go back," I said, looking straight up at the top of the tent. "Things are just going to get worse. This heat like it is—well, it's time."

"No," said Martha. Her eyes were closed, and her hair was wet at the hairline.

"We can't just keep going. It's getting hotter every day, and our money won't last forever. Besides, we'll be at the capital before the week is out. We can't just pitch a tent on the street."

"I'm not going back. There's plenty we haven't seen yet."

I couldn't figure out what she was expecting. Every day now was like another, the sharp gravel beneath us, the fields unrolling without any relief. Every once in a while a car sprayed by, heads inside turning as they passed us. "Then we need to change direction," I said. "We can't just parade into the city. We'll look in the morning to see where we can turn off, which way to go."

"No," said Martha. "We're going north." Stubborn as a tick.

"Martha, it's blazing every day, and there's nothing to look at but corn and fertilizer markers. What're you so sure of finding up this road?"

"I haven't seen everything yet." She was keeping her eyes closed. She knew I wanted her to look at me.

"We can go to the river. You haven't seen that yet, either."

She bunched up her face the way she used to do when she was little, her chin jerking down toward her throat, her lips skinned back from her teeth. "I haven't seen everything on *this* road! You keep turning the way we go. You never ask what I want to see." She started to cry, and she choked on the last words, but she wouldn't open her eyes or even move her head.

"Martha, I ask you all the time."

"You don't! You just wait for me to agree with you so I can get some more birds to come down. I hate birds! They just fly off."

"So what is it you want to see so much? Tractors? Interstates?" I was hot too, and I wanted to shake her. It was all for her, everything we were doing. "Office buildings?"

"I want to see *folks.*" She sounded tight and shrill, like an engine running way too high. "I want to see a farm. You keep me all to yourself, like some damn buried treasure."

"Martha Ruth—" I started. I'd never heard her use language. Then, from outside the tent, someone coughed.

Martha's eyes snapped open like a doll's. The cough happened again, and she smiled, tears puddled in her ears. "Come in," she called before I could even think what to do, and I was sitting with my mouth open when a man stooped his head into the tent.

He wasn't fully a man. There were pimples rimming his mouth, and his hair stuck up on top like pinfeathers. But he was big, crowding us, and he had an unfinished look to him, like stacked lumber. When he smiled he showed that two teeth were gone.

"Is this your land?" I said. "We won't harm anything. It was just so hot, and my sister's sick." Martha, her ears still full of tears, was smiling to beat the band, but I could see the blood pounding at her throat. "We're just out walking," I told him. "We won't cause trouble."

"I know," he said. He shuffled in a little further, propped on his knees and elbows, so he was halfway in the tent with us. His hands were big and loose as slabs of meat.

"We needed rest," I said. "My sister is delicate. Can't abide the heat." I watched him look at her. With her skin so white and her hair, she seemed to be giving off light from the corner where I'd set her down.

"My name is Martha," she said. "That's Janie, my sister."

He wiggled a little further in, grinning his gappy smile. "Earl Hawks." He nodded a little at me, and then he turned back to Martha. "I been watching you."

"I know," said Martha. "I saw you on your combine three days ago."

"Wasn't a combine. 'At's a tractor."

"You were wearing a green cap."

"You got good eyes."

His big hands quivered under his chin as he talked, like the blood in them was running wild. He smelled dusty, and he filled up the tent with heat. I could hardly breathe. I thought sure Martha would keel over, her shrunk lungs frantic for air. "We can move on, if you want us to," I told him. His eyes darted back at me, but he couldn't keep from looking at Martha for long.

"Oh, no," he said. "I came to see you. I wouldn't want you to leave."

"Yes," said Martha. Then she said to me, "Prop me up," like she was some queen, "so Earl Hawks can see." Her eyes were so bright they scared me, and I could feel Earl Hawks watching me as I took

Martha and straightened her, belting her up against her cushion. They kept looking around me to get at each other, and I was thinking we ought to be in somebody's parlor, in a glider on the front porch. Ought to have cookies and lemonade.

"You've been following us," I said.

He grinned at his big hands. "Wasn't hard. But you keep a good pace, considering."

"I saw you," Martha said. "You squatted below the corn when you thought I was looking. Yesterday you disappeared right through the afternoon, and I didn't think you were coming back."

"Went to eat some lunch and got to talking. But I found your trail quick enough."

"This soft gravel's good that way," Martha said. "Holds a trail even in rain, so long as there's not much traffic."

"I wanted to go another way," I announced. I needed to say something. In the glare of their looking I felt blacked out, like the people with no eyes in newspaper ads. "I wanted to go down to the river."

"Janie likes nature," Martha said. "She likes trees."

"I'm a farmer," Earl Hawks said. "Hunnert sixty acres, corn and soybeans. I'm fixing to add another eighty soon."

Martha nodded. "Be fine, if futures hold."

It was TV talk, language from the moon. It was what the man said every morning on the farm report. But we weren't farmers, down in the soft hills that leaned toward Kentucky, and we didn't talk much about futures. "Tinker's damn," I whispered, but I might as well have shouted. It wouldn't have slowed them.

"Got a friend trying to raise cattle. I keep telling him it won't go. This is land for crops. Corn."

"You've got to pay attention to what you want to do," Martha said. "You've got to like what you do."

"I like the look of things growing. Planted right there in the ground."

"Nothing's prettier than corn coming up," Martha said.

I wanted to say, *She's sixteen years old.* She'd never seen a farm a week before. It didn't take any special genius to see what she was thinking, but she wasn't seeing *him*. How he looked at her, his eyes rolling over her seed-shaped body.

"My daddy says pigs," he was saying, "but I don't like them. They can get away from you, and it's hell's own job to get a hog back."

"Feed prices up too," Martha said.

He stayed with us there, half in and half out, until suppertime. It was so hot in the tent that sweat rolled into my eyes and stung, but Earl Hawks and Martha didn't appear to notice. They carried on about farming, living from the land. "I quit school the second I could," Earl Hawks said. "It wasn't teaching me a thing I needed to know. When I was in a classroom on a good planting day, it was pure torture."

Martha tossed her head. "I never went to school a day," she said, and Earl Hawks looked like he worshiped her.

"Is that right," he said.

"I'm a natural kind of person," Martha said. "I don't need people telling me what I'm seeing."

"That's just what I tried to tell them," Earl Hawks said. "Didn't need a book to tell me how to put a seed in the ground. They like to drive me crazy with their charts and such. Forgot it the day I left. Been three years now, and I'm doing all right."

"Some things you're born to," Martha told him. "Some things you just feel in your blood."

What I felt in my blood was heat. It was so dense and wet there in the tent that I felt like a cloud was building, wrapping up Martha and Earl Hawks. I blinked and blinked, but I couldn't get so I could see them. And they kept at it, like kin who've gone years without a word.

"Watch the squirrels, you know when to plant."

"Moon, too."

"Squirrels are better. More of them, so they're steady."

"What about raccoons?" I asked. "Why not just go up and ask them when it's time to plant?" I didn't want to have to just say to Earl Hawks, Don't pay any attention to her. I didn't want to have to say, She's just a kid.

"We don't see raccoons down here," he told me.

"See the moon everyplace," Martha said.

It was another hour before the sun finally began to set and Earl Hawks said, "I suppose I should leave you two to fix your supper."

"Yes," I said, quick, before Martha could say anything. The clothes were sticking to all three of us. I'd been staring I don't know how long at the seam in Earl Hawks' shirt biting into the fleshy underpart of his arm.

"I'd like to walk with you some tomorrow, if that's all right," he said. His hands rose up, pressed down, rose again.

"Yes," Martha shot, glaring at me.

"What about your farm?" I said. "Doesn't it need you?"

"It does. But my daddy can help out for a few days. And I'd sure like to walk with you."

"Come in the morning," Martha said. "Come early."

We walked with Earl Hawks three days. He slept outside the tent, and the morning of the first day he was waiting before we were even decently dressed, and Martha fidgeted and twisted while I sponged her. Earl Hawks was wearing his green cap, and watched while I carried Martha out and fixed her in her chair, and then packed all our gear around her. After I unhooked the brakes he tried to move in front of me, as if he would push. "I've brought us this far," I told him. "I imagine I can keep her going."

"You girls are brave," he said. "No telling the kind of folks you might run into, out on your own like this."

"You're nearly the first folks we've seen," I said.

"Could use some crop rotation over there," Martha said. "Look how puny those stalks are."

It went like that. Martha chattered, busy as a gnat, and Earl Hawks couldn't keep his eyes off her. I watched him, how he agreed with everything she said, every level of foolishness about farming. She brought up fertilizers and land-lease, varieties of weed killers. His eyes went around and around her tiny body, and she grinned and tilted her chin up and tossed her limp hair back. Sixteen years without ever stirring out of the house, and now she was talking about manure, and preening for this farm boy with big hands.

Earl Hawks scratched his head and grinned at her. He looked and looked. He almost walked into fenceposts twice for staring at her. At lunch I made him go away—I didn't want him sitting there while I fed her—but he was back again in twenty minutes, kicking at rocks with his dirty boots, scratching at the ground like a chicken and edging over to where we were sitting.

He wanted to know things, and he wasn't shy about asking. "You get sick much?" he said to her.

"Delicate," I said. "Can't take a lot."

"Mama always said I ran like a watch," Martha said, and I was too surprised to say anything. Who could have guessed she'd remember that?

"Your sister make all your clothes?" he asked her later.

"She buys them ready-made and stitches them," Martha said, looking up sideways at him. "She's handy with a needle. Only thing she never got me is a hat."

Earl Hawks reached up and whipped off his dirty green cap. It said JOHN DEERE across the front, the stitching half gone. "Here. You can have mine."

"Martha Ruth!" I said, looking at her grin under the green cloth, but Earl Hawks interrupted me.

"I want her to have it. I like giving things to people. I met a girl without a hand once, gave her an old awl we had around the place. She got her hand blown off at the paint factory where she was working. Said the woman next to her got blind from paint in her eyes.

" 'Sides," he said. "Sun like this, you need a hat. Maybe she won't be so delicate now." They looked at each other until I pushed the chair again, starting up so hard that everything rattled and the wheels spit gravel behind us.

It was still getting hotter. During the day the sun was dull and grayish, and my hands slipped on the handles of Martha's chair. At night the air was so wet that Martha awakened at midnight soaked, and when I got up to sponge her off I rocked on my feet and saw a quick flood of winking lights.

Our third day with Earl Hawks we took a rest in the afternoon, because we were all three so hot even Martha could hardly muster energy to talk. "Fry an egg on my head," she said faintly, but I don't think Earl Hawks could have heard her. So we sat in the weeds and the Queen Anne's lace and dozed a little. Martha had Earl

Hawks pull the cap down so it rested right over her face, and I curled up in the shade of her chair. I didn't intend to sleep. I just wanted the land to stop wavering and dipping around me. I couldn't keep Martha's and Earl Hawks's faces clear, they kept blending together from all the sweat in my eyes, and their words floated to me in ways that didn't make any sense—"refrigerators," I thought I heard him say, and then she said "aluminum" and "veneer." I heard her say, "It's a showcase design," and that's when I closed my eyes.

I must have dropped off fast because I didn't even hear the car coming. I told myself I would just rest a minute, and there was the heat pressing me down, so even the ants over my legs weren't bothersome. The air was thick, heavy as an animal on my chest. Falling asleep in heat like that is like falling into a soft bag, dark and velvety. I was only there for a few minutes, but it could have been for hours. Could have been until the world came down around me. It took honking and the car fishtailing by for me to jerk awake and see the people in the car all yelling. I jumped right up, and the road and the sky were spinning and I couldn't tell just exactly where the ground was. I grabbed at Martha's chair and closed my eyes for a second, and then I saw colors and lost Martha and everything.

When I opened my eyes again I was flat on the Queen Anne's lace. It was itching like fury on my legs, and Earl Hawks was there, and the car was gone.

"They just wanted some directions," he said when he saw me looking at him. From the ground his eyes were black, and tiny as beads.

"He told them to go straight to hell," Martha said, giggling like she'd been drinking. Her chair was turned so she was facing me, and she had to squint into the sun. The cap was on the ground next to her chair. "They asked him what he was planning to do with me and he told them to go on, that they were seeing things. And then they said I could be a good thing, couldn't fight much, and he told them to go straight to hell."

Earl Hawks looked proud. He smiled and kept bobbing his head, his hands quivering next to Martha. "No call for them to talk like that," he said. "They didn't even know what they were seeing. They were just talking."

"What were they seeing?" I asked. I wasn't thinking about my words. I kept blinking in the sun's bright light, and I was trying to rub out the imprint of weeds on the backs of my legs.

Martha's giggles spilled out, gale force. Earl Hawks kept bobbing and quivering. Then I closed my eyes in earnest, put my face right in my hands that were too wet to bring any comfort. There was dirt on them though, and the grit was something to hold onto when every surface seemed to be hot and slick. "It's time to go back," I said into my hands. "We have to go home. We should have done already."

"I knew she'd say that," Martha said. "I told you she would. I could see it coming."

I rubbed my face with my gritty palms, the dirt scraping over my skin. It was the first thing that had felt right all day.

That night I listened to them. After Martha thought I was asleep, she coughed twice. I heard Earl Hawks slide out the chair and unfold it, and then I heard him feel his way into the tent. *Just don't let him get it wrong,* I was thinking. Because I wouldn't have any choice if he got up, came to me instead. It was too dark in the tent to see anything, but it got hotter with Earl Hawks there, groping around for Martha, and I wished they'd just get it over with. It wasn't like there was anything I could say. I'd spent the whole afternoon trying to find words, but the only ones I could remember were the things I'd said to Martha before we ever left home. "You're a part of the world too," I'd told her, and it was all I could think when I saw Earl Hawks lean down to peck at her cheek the time he thought I wasn't looking.

I stifled the urge to remind him to be sure to get Martha's milk in the morning, to make her drink a lot of water, to brush her hair every day to make it shine. I thought I would hear Earl Hawks grunt when he picked up Martha after he collected her pills and clothes— she was heavier than she looked—but I didn't hear a sound. Just the swish of them brushing against nylon, and they were gone. I stayed perfectly still, waiting for the finger of cool breeze from the flap that Earl Hawks had left up.

I got up before dawn. It took no time at all to leave, just folding the tent and my own clothes. Earl Hawks had left me a knapsack to carry things in since he had the chair. Walking alone in the black air that was already thick as mud, I felt too light, like a dandelion seed. My feet were almost silent on the gravel, and from a distance, I heard a warbler. The light would come soon.

ILLINOIS SHORT FICTION

Pastorale by Susan Engberg
Home Fires by David Long
The Canyons of Grace by Levi Peterson
Babaru by B. Wongar

Bodies of the Rich by John J. Clayton
Music Lesson by Martha Lacy Hall
Fetching the Dead by Scott R. Sanders
Some of the Things I Did Not Do by Janet Beeler Shaw

Honeymoon by Merrill Joan Gerber
Tentacles of Unreason by Joan Givner
The Christmas Wife by Helen Norris
Getting to Know the Weather by Pamela Painter

Birds Landing by Ernest Finney
Serious Trouble by Paul Friedman
Tigers in the Wood by Rebecca Kavaler
The Greek Generals Talk by Phillip Parotti

Singing on the Titanic by Perry Glasser
Legacies by Nancy Potter
Beyond This Bitter Air by Sarah Rossiter
Scenes from the Homefront by Sara Vogan

Tumbling by Kermit Moyer
Water into Wine by Helen Norris
The Trojan Generals Talk by Phillip Parotti
Playing with Shadows by Gloria Whelan

Man Without Memory by Richard Burgin
The People Down South by Cary C. Holladay
Bodies at Sea by Erin McGraw
Falling Free by Barry Targan